"Rule four: no sex. A[...]
lead to sex..."

That's it. Sage had had enough.

If Aiden thought he got to call the shots when it came to her and sex, he was sadly mistaken.

Now it was his turn to learn a thing or two.

Sage smiled. A slow, seductive smile.

Then she got to her feet, her fingers skimming her hips, up her waist before she teased them along the sides of her breasts and up to her throat. Aiden's gaze dropped to her breasts and his own lips tightened. If the fit of his jeans were anything to go by, something else was getting tight, too.

'You go ahead and set those rules," she told him.

'You saying you won't follow them?"

"Rules one through three? I'm one hundred percent committed."

He closed his eyes for a second, then gave her an arch look.

"And rule four?"

"Babe, enforcing that one is all on you." Then, leaning close, she ran her fingertips over his lips before giving him a wide smile.

'Good luck with that..."

Blaze®

Dear Reader,

I am so excited to share Sage and Aiden's story with you for so many reasons. I've always loved fake engagement stories, and even more, friends-to-lovers stories. *A SEAL's Kiss* is both, with a whole lot of sexy SEAL fun thrown in.

One of my favorite parts of this book is the opening chapter. Wedding after wedding after wedding, not only were they fun to write, they were the perfect impetus for Sage's frantic claim that she, too, was getting married. After all, when all your friends are getting married, they tend to look around to see who is left, and immediately go into matchmaking mode. Aiden only goes along with Sage's fake engagement claim out of loyalty to her father, but quickly finds himself in love.

I loved putting Sage and Aiden together. These two are complete opposites who find out that they are more alike than they'd ever imagined. I hope you enjoy their story as much as I enjoyed writing it.

And if you're on the web, I hope you'll stop by and visit! I'll be sharing insider peeks, recipes and contest fun for this story and others on my website at www.tawnyweber.com and on Facebook at www.facebook.com/TawnyWeber.RomanceAuthor.

Happy reading,

Tawny Weber

Tawny Weber

A SEAL's Kiss

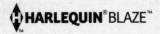

HARLEQUIN® BLAZE™

Recycling programs
for this product may
not exist in your area.

ISBN-13: 978-0-373-79795-0

A SEAL'S KISS

Copyright © 2014 by Tawny Weber

Printed in U.S.A.

ABOUT THE AUTHOR

USA TODAY bestselling author Tawny Weber has been writing sassy, sexy romances since her first Harlequin Blaze book
was published in 2007. A fan of Johnny Depp, cupcakes and
color coordination, she spends a lot of her time shopping
for cute shoes, scrapbooking and hanging out on Facebook.

Visit her website, www.tawnyweber.com, for great contests,
delicious recipes and lots of fun. Or look for her on Facebook
at www.facebook.com/TawnyWeber.RomanceAuthor.

Books by Tawny Weber

To browse a current listing of all Tawny's titles, please visit
www.Harlequin.com.

To the Sassy Sweethearts...

You are all so awesome!

1

Two years ago

WEDDINGS GAVE HER the heebie-jeebies.

Patriarchal rules wearing the pretty mask of traditions and ancient promises that were rarely kept? Definitely not her thing.

A wedding night might be nice, all things considered. Champagne and rose-petal-strewn sex with a man who'd just promised to worship you forever? Not a completely horrible idea.

But to sign your life away to get it? To the same man, day in and day out, 'til death do you part?

Sage Taylor gave a delicate shudder.

She'd rather wear a three-piece suit and give lectures to businessmen on the merits of climbing the corporate ladder through backstabbing, undercutting and sexual favors. Or maybe be staked to an anthill naked while covered in hot fudge.

The only celebrating she wanted that included champagne and rose-petal-strewn sex would come—no pun intended—when she found a guy who could keep it up long enough to worship her until she melted. And who needed forever for that? All she needed was one good night.

Or maybe a weekend.

"What'd you think of the wedding, dear?"

Even though she was pretty sure Mrs. O'Brian couldn't see the naked all-night-sex images playing out in her imagination, Sage still winced.

"It's lovely," Sage said, leaning down so the elderly woman could brush a parchment-dry kiss over her cheek. Not a lie. She'd never lie, especially not to the woman who'd taught her to read. But *lovely* was one of those nice, safe statements that could cover so many things.

Like the weather, with its bright sunshine and cool breeze. Just right for a springtime wedding in a winery.

Or the bride, one of Sage's oldest and dearest friends, who looked so happy she glowed almost as bright as the sunshine.

Or the wine, Sage noted, taking a sip from the glass a passing waiter handed her.

"You made a lovely bridesmaid," Mrs. O'Brian noted, holding her own wineglass up to peer at it with a connoisseur's eye. "I'm sure your father was thrilled to see you at the altar. Any chance you'll be there again soon? Perhaps wearing white?"

"Me? White?" Sage wet her lips, nerves dancing in her stomach. The soft green satin of her bridesmaid dress was as close to wedding accoutrement as she wanted to get. And pretty much as close to wearing white as she warranted. But that wasn't the kind of thing you told a seventy-year-old woman at her niece's wedding. "Um, well..."

"Sage? AnaMaria wants more pictures," Nina Wagner said, tucking her arm through Sage's. The other bridesmaid looked the part much better than Sage ever could. Of course, with her sleek black hair and model looks, Nina was at home in the strapless satin sheath in a way that Sage, with her dreadlocks and multiple piercings, could never appear.

"Ahh, pictures," Mrs. O'Brian said with a wave of her hand. "Go, go. Smile pretty, girls."

Sage went, went, as fast as she could move in the foot-pinching stilettos.

"You looked scared," Nina said, laughing as she pulled Sage across the room toward the buffet.

"She thinks I should be getting married," Sage said, shivering at the thought.

"That is scary." Her arm still tucked tight through her best friend's, Nina laughed even as she scanned the crowd, scoping out the possibilities. Probably looking for a groom of her own.

At her friend's low hum of appreciation, Sage followed her gaze across the room.

As usual, Nina had scoped out the best-looking guy in attendance.

Chief Petty Officer Aiden Masters. Otherwise known as the geeky guy Sage had grown up with.

A protégé of her father's, Aiden was chronologically three years Sage's senior, and mentally thirty years older. But growing up he'd been a social infant compared to her natural ease with people. So while her father had nurtured his mind, she'd figured it her job to keep him from becoming a stodgy old man before he was seventeen. Clearly, from his ease at moving through the crowd, she'd done her job well.

It wasn't just that he was one of the tallest guys there. Or that the contrast of his short black hair and hazel eyes stood out against the vivid white of his military uniform. It was that Aiden Masters was hot.

Under that uniform was a body that sent women into

fantasy mode. Fantasies that, for some bizarre reason, most of them seemed to want to share with Sage. Worse, though, was when one of them managed to make their Aiden fantasy into reality. They liked to share that, too.

Sage was all for reaping the kudos on a job well done, but hearing about Aiden and other women tended to make her teeth hurt.

And the idea of Aiden and Nina?

Um, no.

No way.

Their energies wouldn't match, nor did their personalities. For all her matrimonial goals, Nina was the eat-'em-up-and-toss-them-aside type. And Aiden, well, he might be a navy SEAL, but he still needed protection from some things.

"Aren't we supposed to be joining AnaMaria for pictures?" Sage asked, turning her head toward the bride and groom who were posing under a grapevine arbor across the lawn.

"I just said that to rescue you. Have you already forgotten the cheesy chorus of photos that were taken before the ceremony?"

"How could I?" Happy to have distracted her friend, Sage made a show of grimacing and patting her cheeks to see if they'd recovered from all that smiling yet. She glanced over her shoulder at Mrs. O'Brian. The elderly woman was now in deep conversation with a group of people, giving their wine the same assessing looks, definitely not checking to see if Sage was really getting pictures taken. Still, Sage hated lying. Even little lies, since they were like snowflakes. Put enough of them together and they snowballed. And usually hit you splat in the face when you were least prepared.

As if hearing her thoughts, Nina rolled her eyes, pulled

her cell phone out of the tiny purple purse hanging from her shoulder and wrapped her arm around Sage's waist. Heads together, they smiled pretty and Nina snapped the shot.

"There. You had your picture taken. Now can we get on to the good stuff?"

And this, Sage realized, was what she'd missed about being home. Three months hiking through Tibet was awesome. She'd worked with a charitable organization focused on bringing health care to the women there and had been so touched, she'd written daily blog posts on her website, Sage Advice, that she'd later sold as a series of articles to three magazines to pay for her trip home.

But as great as that'd been, nothing could beat good friends who knew you inside out and had a history that went back to kindergarten.

"What's the good stuff?" Sage asked, still smiling as she inspected the buffet. As to be expected for a Northern California winery wedding, the tables were heavy with appetizers of local produce, cheeses and gourmet delicacies.

"Your love life, of course," Cailley Heath, the third bridesmaid said as she joined them, choosing a juicy red strawberry off the fruit bouquet shaped like a heart. "I want to hear all about sex in Tibet."

"Shhh," Nina hushed. When both Sage and Cailley gave her confused looks, she tilted her head toward the nearby table where two men were sitting, their heads together in serious discussion. Ahh, Aiden had found his other half.

He and Sage's father tended to become inseparable whenever Sailor Boy was on leave. Discussing the latest theory in quantum physics or evidence of an ancient tribe that'd been discovered in a far-off jungle, no doubt.

Sage snickered, then teasingly shook her head at Nina. She could have danced naked with every man in the room right there on their table, and they wouldn't have noticed.

"What?" she teased. "You think my father has no idea I have sex?"

Not that it was a topic of regular discussion. Typical of the Professor, when it was time for the birds-and-bees talk, her widowed father had a local nurse chat with Sage, filling her in on all of the pertinent details.

After which her friends had filled her in on the juicy ones.

"Your dad might know you have sex," Cailley teased. "But does Aiden?"

"I'm sure he does," Sage said with an exasperated roll of her eyes, pretending the words *her, Aiden* and *sex* in the same sentence didn't send a naughty thrill to all the wrong places. "The real question is, why would he care?"

"I dunno. The way he looks at you sometimes is pretty intense," Cailley said, her tone turning serious enough to make Sage twitchy. She shrugged it off, though. Aiden didn't look at her as anything other than a friend. A flaky, weird friend whose father was his mentor.

"He always looks intense. That's just Aiden," Sage said dismissively, focusing on the buffet instead. With all the choices, she wanted to try a little of everything here. Which would be much more satisfying than talking about a guy who even found ways to straighten the straight and narrow.

"Just as well," Nina replied, filling her own plate with salad, no dressing. "A sexy SEAL might be fun for a fling, but he'd definitely be a bad idea for the long term. I want a guy who'll be around all the time. Ready and willing to fulfill my every wish."

Sage laughed, but Cailley gave a dissatisfied grunt.

"You've always known exactly what you want," the blonde said with a heavy sigh.

True. While Sage had no idea what she wanted, and bounced from idea to idea, first in her one-year attempt at college, then later in her varied and sundry jobs throughout the country.

But Nina was totally focused on exactly what she wanted. After graduation, it'd been to get into UC Davis. After college, it'd been to get a job as a viticulture researcher at the local winery. And now, at twenty-five they all knew getting married was next up on Nina's schedule.

"You know what you want," Nina said in a soothing tone.

"I don't think *move out of my mom's apartment* and *find a job that pays enough to cover my student loans* is exactly knowing what I want," Cailley said, her lower lip shifting into a pout.

Poor Cailley. Unlike Sage, who was happy to move on to the next job when one didn't fit, Cailley was desperately trying to find that perfect match.

"Hey, I met this guy last week who used to work as a headhunter for a big corporation," Nina said, snapping her fingers. "He's got lots of training in career counseling. You should talk with him."

Her pout forgotten, Cailley gave an excited yes.

"How about you, Sage? Did you want to talk to him while you're home, too?" Nina offered tentatively.

"A career counselor? No, but thanks," Sage refused with a laugh, taking her filled plate to a small table and settling in to enjoy the meal.

"You really should. If you don't, you'll just keep bouncing around, not getting ahead."

"I'm fine with that. There is so much out there to see and do and explore." The possibilities were endless. She wanted to find something that touched her soul. That made her spirit sing. All she had to do was keep looking until she found it. "Why dismiss any of the possibilities until I've tried them all?"

"Is that what you say about the guys?" Nina joked.

"Only until she finds the right guy," Cailley tossed in. "As soon as that happens, Sage will settle down fast."

Settle down? As in, quit searching for her bliss? Live in one place, for the rest of her life? Do the same thing day in and day out?

Sage shuddered. If that wasn't incentive to avoid that particular guy, she didn't know what was.

One year ago

"Seriously? A twenties-themed wedding?" Sage adjusted her headband, which kept trying to slide over her forehead, making her look like a drunken goth-style flapper. At least her bridesmaid dress was black, the beads glinting in the candlelight to match the blue tips of her razor-cut black hair. "What was Cailley thinking?"

"Well, Eric proposed at that Johnny Depp gangster movie, so they thought it'd be a fun, romantic way to commemorate it," AnaMaria said, looking much more suited to the flapper theme with her cute red curls and matching lipstick. "You missed all the pre-wedding fun though. They had a Bonnie-and-Clyde-style picnic, complete with vintage cars and barbecue yesterday."

"I feel horrible about that, too," Sage said with a grimace. "I'd have loved to see the cars. My dad was talking about it all the way from the airport this morning."

She didn't want to admit that she'd barely made it for the wedding at all. Dave, her boyfriend until last week, had hocked her original plane ticket that would have gotten here a week ago. She'd found out the night before her flight was due to leave, then had had to work overtime at the coffee bar all week, call in a few favors and borrow against her next paycheck to replace it. She'd covered the last-minute fare difference by selling Dave's drum set.

She'd thought she wanted a guy who needed her. That maybe being a part of helping him find his passion was her way to bliss. But there wasn't much bliss to be found in giving a wannabe diva a free ride.

"So what's the deal?" AnaMaria asked quietly after a few seconds.

"Deal?" Sage prevaricated. Sharing the fact that she'd just ended yet another unfulfillingly dead-end, soul-dimming relationship wasn't her idea of wedding fun.

"Yeah. The deal. Just a month ago you were talking about how fun this visit was going to be. Two weeks ago, in between your call for donations to the animal shelter, you blogged about introducing the boyfriend to your friends. So...where's the hot rock-star boyfriend? Why weren't you here a week ago? And why do you look so bummed?" Clearly out of breath, but not questions, AnaMaria filled her lungs and looked like she was going to keeping going.

Sage held up one hand before the other woman said anything else and shook her head. This was a sitting-down sort of conversation, so she glanced around.

"Let's chill," she suggested, waving her hand to indicate one of the small tables in the corner.

"I don't think the Seattle scene is really me," she admitted when they were settled. She ran her fingers over the smooth satin tablecloth, letting the fabric cool her stress. "I thought I wanted something intense, you know. The rock scene, music, the passion of it. But I'm not finding what I need there."

"Dave wasn't passionate enough?" AnaMaria asked,

scooting her chair closer and leaning her head in, making it clear that she was ready to hear any and all naughty details.

And oh, the details they were. Sage pressed her lips together, then shrugged. Why not? She hadn't come away with much from the relationship, she might as well have fun now.

"He was passionate about his music. So much so that he could only get it up if his tunes were playing in the background," she dished, leaning close to offer a wicked smile and a wriggle of her brows. "And mirrors. He liked doing it in front of mirrors."

AnaMaria's mouth rounded into an O.

"Well, that's kinda sexy, right?" the redhead asked, her cheeks as bright as her hair now. "At least, I've heard it is."

It was all Sage could do not to hug her close. For a woman married well over a year to a pretty hot cop, AnaMaria was awfully sheltered.

"The mirrors—plural, by the way—were always angled so he could focus on just him." It'd been sexy the first time. Interesting the next few as she watched him flex and preen. Sorta like watching her own personal porn film. But the novelty had faded fast.

"Mirrors? Oh my." Looking baffled, and a little intrigued, AnaMaria waved to the passing waiter, indicating she wanted whatever appetizers he was passing out. When it turned out to be stuffed mushrooms and bacon-wrapped scallops, Sage took a plate as well.

"But he was deep in the rock scene, right? You said you couldn't wait to bask in the creative energy and grungy vibe," AnaMaria asked after a few bites.

Sage's lips twitched, wondering if it'd taken her friend all that time to find a safe response, or if she'd been trying to envision a guy who preferred sex with himself.

"In the four months we were together, he joined and

left five bands, went through twelve tubes of eyeliner and had to be talked out of jumping off our first-floor balcony three times."

"First-floor…"

"Balcony," Sage finished, taking a glass of champagne from another passing waiter. "He liked the drama, but wasn't a fan of anything physical. Like pain. Or work."

"Except sex with mirrors," AnaMaria intoned, grinning before sipping her own champagne.

"Exactly," Sage agreed, figuring it was better to laugh through the pain. It was that or cry.

Was it too much to want a guy who was dedicated to what he did, had that deep passion for life—and the ability to please a woman without using strange kink? If he just had that, she'd put up with all of the negative qualities. Because if she was learning nothing else on this quest she called life, it was that everyone came with negatives. The trick was to find people who had more positives to balance that out.

Too bad she wasn't having much luck on that score. She drained her glass in a single gulp, the bubbles hitting her fast.

"Sage, I want you to meet someone," Nina said, her words as bright as her excited smile. The brunette slid into an empty chair and helped herself to a mushroom from AnaMaria's plate. "He's really cute, smart and single. You'll love him."

"How'd you know she's single?" AnaMaria asked, shifting her plate farther out of reach. "Just a week ago she was sharing the awesomeness that was her rocker-boy."

"He's not here, is he?"

"So? That doesn't mean anything where Sage is concerned. She never brings guys home. Even when she says she will, she finds a way to avoid it."

"You're right," Nina said, her tone contemplative as they both turned searching looks on Sage. "Why do you think that is? Maybe she's ashamed of us?"

"More likely she doesn't want her guy to know she comes from such a normal upbringing."

"Or perhaps she knows you'll make inappropriate comments and embarrass us all," Sage interrupted, rolling her eyes.

"There is that," Nina acknowledged with a big smile, taking her next bite off of Sage's plate. "So? What do you say?"

"To what?"

"To meeting this guy."

"A fix-up?" Sage asked, cringing.

"Not a fix-up. A date while you're home. What?" Nina said, her expression as innocent as she could make it. "Were you going to hide at your dad's the entire visit?"

"I hadn't really thought about it." She hadn't actually thought past where she'd snag some work to buy herself a plane ticket back to Seattle. Even though it was time to move on, she still had to pack up.

And figure out where she wanted to go next.

"So, give Jeffrey a chance while you're here. A date or two. What's the harm? You might find out you like him."

"What's he do?"

"He's a doctor."

AnaMaria laughed at the horror on Sage's face.

"Um, no, thank you," Sage said, waving both palms in the air to indicate the end of that train of thought.

"Why not? You've already tried the Indian chief. You might as well give a lawyer and a doctor a try."

"He wasn't a chief. He was a fire dancer," Sage muttered. "And I'm not interested in professional guys. You know that."

"I don't see why not," Nina muttered before launching into a soliloquy about this guy's glowing traits.

Barely listening, Sage's eyes cut across the hall to her father, who was drinking scotch and chatting with the groom's father. As usual, it was weird to see the Professor without a book in hand. Her earliest memories were of him reading to her. She'd spent her toddler years after her mother had died playing at his feet while he worked at his desk, at home or at the university.

Her every memory of her father was colored by his dedication to learning. His avocation for amassing and honoring knowledge. A worthy goal, and something she was very proud of him for.

But that didn't mean he was the kind of guy she wanted to spend the rest of her life with. Been there, done that. She wanted spiritual instead of cerebral.

"Give him a chance," Nina persuaded. "He's really cute. And isn't it time you tried someone new?"

"Like guys are flavors of ice cream?"

"Hey, you're the one who's vowed to avoid vanilla."

"C'mon, Nina," AnaMaria said, nudging their friend with her shoulder. "If Sage wanted a guy like her dad, she'd just hook up with Aiden Masters. He's got all those qualities going on, plus he's got the best body of any guy who's ever come out of Villa Rosa."

They all paused for a second to pay mental homage to Aiden's hot body, then Nina waved her hand through the air as if dispersing the image from everyone's mind.

"Aiden isn't here. And he's not Sage's type. Jeffrey is here, and while he might not be the type Sage has gone for in the past, he could be now."

"No," Sage decided adamantly. "Maybe I haven't figured out what kind of guy is perfect for me yet. But I do know what kind isn't perfect. As much as I adore my father, I don't want a guy like him. Dedication, focus and intensity are all well and good. But I want more than that. I want passion and creativity and drama."

"Drama leads to guys jumping off the first-floor balcony," AnaMaria reminded her.

Ugh. Good point. But Sage shrugged it off, focusing instead on the delight of building her vision.

"I want a guy who makes me shiver with his insights," she expanded, staring at the white wall as if the image of that guy would coalesce there. "One who has excitement and dedication and a soul-deep hunger for exploring the depths of the human experience."

AnaMaria and Nina exchanged glances, then Nina shook her head.

"If I were you, I'd settle on great sex."

"Sex?" Sage repeated with a baffled look. How could Nina equate sex to a spiritual nirvana?

"Sure. With the right guy, you'll get all of that and an orgasm. Shivers, excitement, and deep exploration. What more does a girl want?"

Sage contemplated the last few months of mirror-focused sex and sighed.

What more, indeed.

Two weeks ago

"After all of your years of plotting and planning, of saving bridal magazines and making lists, you eloped?"

"A girl's gotta do what a girl's gotta do," Nina said, looking so content Sage couldn't even teasingly chide her. "Besides, I didn't think you could get back until summer and I didn't want to wait that long to become Mrs. Jeffrey Philips."

"I can't believe you married my doctor," Sage said,

laughing as she wandered through Nina's new living room. Filled with thick carpets, rich wood and silk-covered furniture, it was posh to say the least. She wasn't surprised that after less than two weeks her friend had already unpacked and settled in. Nina was good at that.

"Well, you weren't going to date him. I figured I'd give it a try," Nina said, stretching out on the divan with a contented look on her face.

"You said you'd never marry a guy who had a job that might come before you, remember? I can't imagine a doctor doesn't put his career in the top slot."

Nina's shrug was as luxurious as the room itself. Clearly priorities were adjustable if the bank account was big enough.

Hey, that might not be her way, but Sage couldn't fault her friend. At least she knew what she wanted. Unlike some people who had spent over a decade claiming they knew what they wanted—even if whatever that was changed from year to year.

Sage pushed her hand through her hair, recently dyed back to her original golden-blond. After three months of bouncing from job to job in Sedona, Arizona—the woowoo capital of the desert—she'd finally accepted that she actually had no idea what she wanted. Or where she wanted it.

So she'd done what anyone would do. She'd slinked home without a word to anyone. She'd hoped to sneak into her father's house and hide until she'd figured out what was missing from her life. But she'd run into the new Dr. and Mrs. Philips at the airport, of all places.

"You realize now that I'm settled, you're the last one of our circle still single," Nina pointed out, inspecting her manicure as if checking to see if she were up to the coming task of taking care of that little problem.

"No. No, no, no," Sage protested, sinking into the chair

opposite her friend and offering a look of horror. "No fix-ups. You married the last guy you tried to fix me up with, which should tell you how bad you are at matchmaking."

"I have other guys in mind this time," Nina informed her. "I've been making a list since Cailley's wedding."

That sounded ominous enough to send a chill down Sage's spine. A list that long meant Nina was determined. A determined Nina was a pain-in-the-ass Nina. And Sage just couldn't deal with it right now.

Not while she was fighting the horrible suspicion that everyone had been right about her for years. That, instead of being a free spirit in search of bliss, she was really a wishy-washy flake who'd never be satisfied with anything.

"That's sweet of you to think of me," Sage said quickly. "But I'm not available."

"Of course you are."

"No. I'm not."

Nina gave a pitying click of her tongue, as if Sage thinking she had any say in this was funny.

"You need a guy. I'm going to find you one. The perfect one," Nina stated. "Even if we have to go through dozens to get there. Which is fine, since I have a lot of options on my list."

Good God. Sage shuddered. She had to stop this. Now. There was no way she was going to get her head together and figure out why her life was so blah if she was fending off blind dates.

"I'm not available," she insisted. Maybe if she pretended to have a boyfriend, Nina would leave her alone.

"Why? Because you're dating some schmo who you'll dump in two weeks? That's fine. I can wait."

"He's not a schmo. He's a great guy. The perfect guy." After all, why would she date an imaginary guy who wasn't perfect?

"Who?"

Sage shrugged, trying to look coy while her mind raced. She wanted Nina off her back, or she'd be fending off fix-ups from her, AnaMaria and Cailley until she left town. But she was lousy at lying. She was a great dancer, though, so hopefully sidestepping would be enough.

"Is it serious?"

"I wouldn't say serious," Sage prevaricated.

"Then you are okay to date other guys."

"Although we are talking marriage." The words flew off Sage's tongue before her brain even realized they were an option.

She wanted to grab them back. *Marriage?* Her? Nina was sure to laugh in her face, grab her phone and arrange Sage's first fix-up date before she'd even unpacked.

Before she could grab, or think up a better lie to cover up her first lie, Nina flew into a sitting position, going from mellow to shocked in a single breath.

"Who? Who's the guy?" Eyes narrowed, Nina shook her head. "The perfect guy, who you're crazy enough about to stick with for more than five minutes, and willing to consider marrying, which means introducing him to your father and friends."

She made it sound like that guy didn't exist.

Sage frowned. She might have a point.

Then, like a lightbulb flashing on, she had it.

"Aiden." She gave Nina a triumphant smile. "Aiden Masters and I are engaged."

FEELING A LITTLE SMUG and a lot relieved to be off the match-making hit list, Sage walked into her dad's house, calling his name as she moved through the rooms.

She'd emailed last night to tell him she'd be here today. When she'd gone straight from the airport to Nina's, she'd texted to let him know she'd be a few hours. His lack of reply hadn't worried her. He always read her notes, but rarely replied.

But his lack of presence in his own house was starting to make her twitch.

She reached the study and stopped short, frowning.

She always found him in the study, buried in books, papers and his own brilliant thoughts.

Where was he?

"Dad?" she called again, heading back to the front of the house. "Are you here?"

"Sage?" Coming from the kitchen, her father pushed a hand through his hair, sounding confused. "When did you get home? I wasn't expecting you."

She opened her mouth, but nothing came out.

It'd only been eight months since she'd seen him. What had happened? He looked horrible. Like he'd lost weight, color and half his life force. Her feet felt like they were glued to the floor with dread as he shuffled over to wrap his arms around her. Instead of being engulfed in the usual bear hug, it was like being patted down by a skeleton. And what did he mean, he wasn't expecting her? Her frown deepened and a heavy knot took hold deep in her belly.

Before she could comment, another man joined them in the foyer.

"Dr. Brooke?" she said in greeting, sounding as confused as she felt. She thought that while her father respected their neighbor as a skilled oncologist, he also considered the guy as boring as dried mud. Now they were coffee buddies?

"Sage, I'm glad you're home," the doctor said, his expression gravely relieved.

"What's going on?"

She looked from her father to the doctor then back again.

"Dad?"

"Sweetie, I'll explain everything," he promised, patting her icy hand. Despite his horrible appearance, he looked like he'd just won the lottery, discovered a time machine and had spent the weekend with a roomful of exotic dancers, combined. His huge smile was at direct odds with the dread in her belly.

"But first, sweetie, I want all the details of your great news. I hear we're having a wedding."

2

The present

AHH, VILLA ROSA.

He'd been gone quite a while. Two tours and his last couple leaves spent in sunny places meant he hadn't been back in well over a year. Long enough that Chief Petty Officer Aiden Masters wondered why he still considered Villa Rosa home. Or if he did.

For a guy that spent most of his life on a naval base, transferring from the east to the west coast and back and called an APO his mailing address, home was an odd concept.

There were plenty of odes to coming home in literature. Hell, Odysseus had spent two decades obsessed with the task. Movies were sold on the theme month after month. People made a big deal out of it all the time.

But for Aiden, coming home was a mystery. Was he supposed to feel nostalgia over crossing the city limits of Villa Rosa, just because he'd spent time here as a kid? Or was that special feeling reserved for the little corner of Idaho he'd been born in, even though he hadn't been there since he was two? Was familiarity a qualifier to calling a place his own? Was it longevity, since he'd lived here longer than any other place? Maybe the fact that he owned a little cottage on the outskirts of Villa Rosa? More for a place to store his parents' things than because he wanted a tax write-off.

Whatever it was, it wasn't sentiment. Aiden was too smart to make decisions based on vague feelings of longing or silly emotions.

Yet, that morning he'd left Coronado Naval Base with a vague plan to take the first plane heading somewhere hot. But he'd hit the airport, and found himself asking for a ticket to San Francisco instead. From there, he'd rented a car and drove the three hours north.

And he still wasn't sure why.

He just knew something was missing, off.

What, he hadn't figured out.

Yet.

Driving through the narrow, familiar streets, Aiden watched the people, recognizing many of them. So if he was home, as per some definitions of the concept, why was he still so unsatisfied? What the hell was wrong with him?

Stopped at a red light, he scrubbed one hand over his face and sighed. Or maybe he'd just sleep. Damn, he was tired. This last mission had been a bitch. Rough enough to have him entertaining the rare thought of hanging up his naval uniform and doing something else.

Something chill.

Like sleeping.

That could be the fact that other than zoning out on the hour-long flight, he hadn't had any shut-eye in about two days. No biggie. Aiden was used to operating at peak efficiency under less-than-ideal circumstances.

Still, sleep would be good.

Or maybe his bunkmate, Castillo, had been right when he'd told Aiden to go get laid on leave.

Sex had definite appeal.

But sex in Villa Rosa? Not such a hot idea.

He returned a couple of waves, even though he didn't know the people's names. Of course, they probably didn't know his either. In a town the size of Villa Rosa, waves didn't tend to be personal. They were more a random greeting offered to friend and stranger alike. Or a warning that yes, they'd seen his vehicle and were noting his license number. Just in case.

Or maybe too much time in the Middle East, facing distrust, destruction and despair had gotten to him.

Maybe that's why he'd felt the need to see this place. Because nothing in his life was personal, and he was starting to wonder why.

Including sex.

His stomach growled, making itself heard over the Stones pounding out of the radio. A timely reminder that once he reached the cottage, his cupboards were gonna be bare.

So when the light turned green, he turned left instead of going straight, deciding to get a few things to tide him over. At least until tomorrow, when he'd visit the Professor and get some real food.

Thinking of the old guy made him smile. It'd be good to catch up. Visit. Talk about things that required brains, not brawn. Get his ass kicked at chess and expand his mind a little. He could always count on Professor Lee Taylor for all of that.

Parking in front of the small grocer's, Aiden pocketed the keys and headed for beer and cereal. All he'd need, he decided, to last until he could hit the old guy up for eggs Benedict in the morning.

"Well, well, look at the soldier boy."

Aiden glanced over as a bruiser the size of Lieutenant Castillo and twice as ugly sauntered over. It took less than a second to place him. Two years older than Aiden and three grades behind, the star of the football team had a reputation for being an ass to the ladies.

"Aren't you supposed to wear a little white uniform or something, Soldier Boy?" the guy asked as he reached Aiden.

"That's sailor, not soldier, and I'm off duty," Aiden responded quietly, sliding the guy a sideways glance that didn't pack any more punch than he'd offer any other asshole who was in his way.

The guy blinked a couple of times, then shifted a step to the right, putting a little distance between them and lifted both hands as if in surrender.

"Dude, no offense. Just wanted to stop you and say congratulations," the guy said, slapping Aiden on the back. His just-this-side-of-nasty grin and the extra force of that slap were in keeping with Aiden's memory of him being a dickhead. "You caught yourself a wild one. Good luck taming her."

Taming who?

Aiden didn't ask, though. He had a policy against engaging dickheads. Instead, he offered a dismissive smile and kept moving toward the grocery store.

He didn't make it through the automatic doors before he was grabbed by a very large, very plush woman who he thought he might have taken a piano lesson from once in first grade.

Before he could ask what the hell was up, she started babbling and blubbering at the same time, pulling him into a hug that smelled like cinnamon rolls.

"Oh, Aiden, I'm so happy for you. Congratulations. You're a lucky man." She leaned back to pat his cheeks with both of her plump hands, smiling so wide he didn't have the heart to let her know she was crazy. "After all this time, you'll have a family again. Such a blessing."

He'd been seventeen when his parents were killed. He was thirty years old now. Hardly a helpless orphan then, or now. So what was she talking about, he'd have a family? Afraid to find out, Aiden smiled instead and mumbled a thanks. His stomach growling, he quickly extricated himself and headed into the store.

A minute later, six-pack in hand, he headed for the cereal aisle.

"Aiden? Aiden Masters?"

Hanging his head, wondering why he'd thought Villa Rosa was a good place to rest, Aiden sighed then turned. A little of the edgy exhaustion faded at the sight of Sergeant Gary Davis, a local cop and a great guy.

The two men came together in a solid chest-bumping hug, shaking hands and grinning at each other as they took stock of how each had held up over time.

"I haven't seen you since you stood as best man at my wedding."

Right. Gary had married that little redhead, AnaMaria.

"What's that been? Two years," Aiden calculated. "I wanted to make it back last year for Eric's wedding but I was on duty."

On a rescue mission gone miserably wrong, Aiden remembered. They'd lost one guy, almost lost another to the aftereffects. He ground his teeth at the memory, trying to shrug off the tight bands of stress gripping him. Brody Lane was back on duty, engaged to be married, even. The team was solid. Carrying the weight of missions past only weighed on a guy, Aiden knew. So, as he always did, he made himself focus on the here and now.

Which was his high school buddy, who was nodding,

his grin widening as if he were thinking of just how good those couple of married years had been.

"Guess we'll be celebrating your wedding soon, right?"

Huh? Aiden squinted, wondering if his old friend had taken a few head shots. He'd have thought Villa Rosa was a pretty mellow place, but you never knew.

"I'm impressed," Gary said, shaking his head as if baffled was a better term. "If there was a pool over whom everyone thought was least likely to marry, I swear it'd have been a tie between the two of you. And now you're getting together?"

Again…huh? A surreptitious sniff assured him that Gary hadn't taken to drinking on the job.

So what the hell was he talking about?

Before Aiden could ask, the radio on Gary's belt crackled. The sergeant responded, then gave Aiden a *gotta go* look.

"Congrats, man," his buddy said as he headed down the aisle. "I know some people think she's a little weird, with all the traveling and crazy jobs she's had. But she and AnaMaria are tight, so I know how great she really is. And her father must be thrilled. He's always had a soft spot for you."

A thrilled father. Crazy jobs and traveling.

No longer needing to ask what everyone was talking about, Aiden's gaze shifted to the front of the grocery store, where he could see the highest hill in Villa Rosa through the gleaming plate glass.

Sage.

As always, just her name invoked a gutful of mixed feelings. Exasperation, affection, lust.

Damn, what'd she done this time?

Handing the beer to a passing stock boy, Aiden made

a beeline for the exit, not stopping to talk to anyone on the way to his car.

Professor Lee Taylor had been a lifesaver to a ten-year-old brainiac geek with more IQ points than social skills, who was too advanced even for the gifted program. Realizing that ten was just too young to take classes alongside college students, the Professor had created a special curriculum and tutored Aiden himself. He'd shown Aiden the thrill of expanding his brain, of accepting his mental skills. He'd welcomed him into his home, first at fifteen when Aiden hadn't wanted to follow his parents to New York, then at seventeen when his parents had been killed in the Twin Towers. He'd provided a touchstone, been a mentor and always given Aiden a sense of acceptance.

And then there was his daughter, Sage.

Three years Aiden's junior, she was about as opposite in personality of her father as the sun was from the moon. But like the Professor, she'd welcomed Aiden into their family with a no-strings open-armed sort of acceptance. Despite her father's focus on his protégé, she'd never shown any jealousy. Rather, she'd seemed relieved that her dad had found someone like Aiden, taking the pressure off of her.

As a thanks for that, she'd spent a good portion of the last two decades driving him crazy.

So Aiden no longer questioned why people thought he and Sage were engaged. He knew the prodigal daughter must be home and for reasons probably only clear to herself, was up to something. He just had to find out what.

And then decide what he wanted to do about it.

Knowing better than to prejudge, or even try to guess about anything Sage did, he kept his mind clear of questions as he made his way up the hill to the Taylor house. He parked behind a handful of cars in the circular driveway. As soon as he opened his door the sound of laughter and splashing water hit him.

Not bothering with the front door, he made his way around the house toward the pool. Set a few hundred yards away from the house, the Professor had built the waterfall-inspired feature as a treat for his daughter when she'd decided she wanted to be a mermaid. Not to swim, or for sunbathing. That wasn't whimsical enough for Sage.

And knowing his daughter's love of socializing—something that baffled both the Professor and Aiden alike—he'd built it big, with ample room for entertaining and a large gazebo at one end.

It was around that white open-aired building that most of the crowd gathered.

And there, like the most exotic flower in the garden, was Sage. Aiden had a special radar when it came to her. Call it an eye for trouble, or the fact that despite his best efforts to keep her out, she always snuck into his sexiest fantasies. It didn't matter that she looked nothing like the last time he'd seen her, or that her back was to him, it didn't take him more than a glance to pick her out of the crowd.

Rather than pitch-black and edgy, her hair was back to her natural blond, waving halfway down her back. Even from behind, her tall, slender frame was as familiar to him as his own. And her laugh rang out, the welcome home he hadn't realized he was waiting for.

As usual, she was surrounded by people. A few he recognized from the social events he'd attended from time to time while home on leave. A few he knew from school.

None of them mattered.

It was hard to pay attention to anything, anyone, since Sage was wearing a bikini.

A couple of teeny, tiny turquoise scraps of fabric that covered little, but did a great job of drawing attention to the curves between the material.

When whoever she was talking to gestured, Sage quickly turned.

Aiden desperately hoped his moan was only in his head and not aloud. Because oh, baby, she was gorgeous.

Her breasts filled the bikini top with a generous bounty, her curves an ode, he knew, to her yoga discipline and not any sort of diet. Already pale gold, despite it only being spring, her skin seemed to glow. To beckon. His fingers itched to touch.

His desperate need for her always took him by surprise. As was his habit whenever he saw her again, he had to warn himself to keep his distance. No touching, no lusting. He knew from experience that it'd only take a few minutes, an hour tops, before the message sank in.

All that SEAL training for command over his body came in handy for this kind of thing.

Because Sage Taylor was strictly off-limits.

As if hearing and mocking his thoughts, she clapped her hands together with her usual exuberance at the sight of him and hurried barefoot across the lawn.

The crowd followed.

At least, Aiden thought it did. There was a blur of bodies moving behind her bikini-clad form. But he was so busy trying not to drool and commanding his erection to stand down that he wasn't positive.

Damn, she had gorgeous legs.

"Aiden," she called when she was a few yards away. Her smile as wide as her legs were long, she threw out both arms as if to hug him from across the yard. "I didn't realize you were coming home."

There was something there beneath the bright smile and enthusiastic tone. But before he could figure out what, she was close enough that her scent wrapped around him. A mix of fresh grass, some sort of incense and the faint aroma of flowers.

"I hear you're causing trouble again," he said in lieu of a greeting. "Isn't that always more fun if I'm here to appreciate it?"

"Me?" she asked with a laugh, pressing one hand against her lush chest and making him want to whimper. "When have I ever caused trouble?"

"When haven't you?" he responded with a grin of his own.

"I'm innocent, I tell ya," she claimed as she reached him.

"Right. Like I'm dumb enough to believe that?" He fell into the easy, teasing banter, knowing the faster they re-established those friendly boundaries, the faster his body would get the message.

"Aww, you sweet talker, you." Her eyes, a few shades lighter than her swimsuit, danced with glee. But they were shadowed, hinting at worry and stress. Two things he'd never associated with Sage.

"What's wrong?" he asked quietly, glancing behind her at the people slowly making their way toward them.

"Like I said, I didn't realize you were going to be home so soon," she told him, frowning a little as she too looked at her posse.

Since he hadn't realized he was coming home either until that morning when he'd changed his flight from Aruba to San Francisco, he was sure that was true. But that wasn't what was bothering her.

"Sage?"

"I'm sorry, babe," she said, a hint of something in her husky tone that put his senses on full alert. "I know you wanted to keep it a secret. But I'm so bad at that kind of thing, and when Dad asked, I just had to tell him our news."

"What news—" Before he could finish his very reasonable question, Sage threw herself into his arms with enough force to catch him by surprise.

Not over the move.

He'd come to expect anything and everything from his mentor's daughter over the years.

But over the desperation that had her body tight and her hands shaking as they curved over his shoulders. She was in trouble. And not simple trouble, this time. His body tensed, his hands going to her waist as much to comfort as to hold her in place so he could inspect her face.

As soon as he touched her, tiny explosions of need shot through him. Ignoring them, he tried to read her expression and figure out why she was pretending to be happy when she looked so deeply miserable.

Lucky for him his body was good at multitasking.

"What's going on?" he asked, his words low.

He looked at the small crowd gathered behind her. Before he could ask why everyone was wearing a cheesy grin and staring like he'd just won a Nobel Prize, Sage moved even closer.

Plastered that sweet—oh, God, she felt so sweet—body against his in a way guaranteed to command his full attention.

Then, before he could push her away or even demand an explanation for the crazy public behavior, she planted that full, usually babbling mouth on his.

And Aiden forgot everything.

His demand for information.

His reasonable argument.

Her tongue slid, hot and tempting, over the seam of his lips.

And he straight-up forgot his own name.

YUM.

Aiden Masters wasn't just hot to look at, Sage realized as she sank into the hard expanse of his chest.

He was hot to kiss, too. And tasty.

Her mouth moved over his with as much curiosity as delight.

How much had he learned in the last ten years?

And how much of that learning would he be willing to show her? Despite the way his body had stiffened—and not in a way that a girl hoped for—she still wanted to find out.

Mmmm. She let the sensations sweep over her, breathing in Aiden's scent, crisp and heady over the smell of chlorine and fresh-mown lawn. Her fingers slid, just a little desperate, over the round hardness of his biceps, and she shivered a little wondering what else he had that might be just as hard.

This was Aiden. They were friends, which meant there were boundaries that should be respected. That she shouldn't be thinking this kind of thing about him, or doing this kind of thing to him, didn't matter. This was for show, and sometimes putting on a show meant getting into the role. Besides, her body was desperate for a distraction, her mind more than willing to shut down its freaked-out thoughts while she reveled in a little sensual delight.

Before she could revel too much, or find out what other hard things he had to offer, Aiden pulled away. She almost pouted at the loss of his mouth. The cool sweep of air made her shiver as he put distance between their bodies.

Before she could protest, or do anything else that would most likely embarrass them both, Aiden tilted his head behind her. As if freed from a spell, the murmurs and laughter of her guests hit her with a reminder of why she'd blurred that boundary.

"We should talk," she said in a low, husky whisper, hoping anyone who heard would take it as sexy talk.

"Ya think?" His words were pure sarcasm, but the indulgent amusement in Aiden's hazel eyes warmed her like a friendly hug. He might be irritated, and with good reason, but he'd go along.

She had to get him alone to explain, though.

Which wouldn't be easy, she admitted as they were suddenly surrounded by people.

Nerves, something she'd rarely felt until this last week, gripped tight. Sage took a deep breath, trying to envision soothing energy pouring over her. But between the expression on Aiden's face and the bodies crowding around, all she got was more nerves.

Didn't it figure that the one day she'd been unable to handle the company of her own thoughts any longer, Aiden showed up. This meeting—and explanation—would have been so much easier without an audience.

"Hey, I'm gonna steal Aidan away for a while," she said, turning to face the crowd with her fingers tightly wound around his. To everyone else it probably looked like they were holding hands. But Sage, and probably Aiden, knew it was to keep him from stealing himself away.

"Lovebirds."

"So cute."

"Don't do anything I wouldn't do."

Sage rolled her eyes, gripping Aiden tighter when she felt him start to pull away.

"You guys don't mind, do you?" she asked, her tone making it clear that it didn't matter if they did or not. "Go ahead and enjoy the pool. We'll join you later. Maybe."

With that, and to a roar of laughter and suggestive words, she tucked her arm into Aiden's and pulled—or yanked, rather—him around the house toward the lanai.

"Wonder who'll teach who the most? The soldier boy or the party girl?"

She tugged harder on Aiden's arm when his footsteps slowed, not sure if he were more likely to take offense at being called a soldier instead of a sailor, or the implication that she was a slut.

Probably the slut thing. Aiden had beat a kid up in the fifth grade for calling her stupid. Then there was the time in high school when some guy had thought there was a direct correlation between Sage studying art and her need to see guys naked.

"C'mon," she murmured. "Just ignore them."

"You gonna fill me in on the reason for the dumbass remarks?"

"Mine? Or theirs? Because I can only truly explain my own actions," she said, keeping her tone light and teasing as she continued to pull him around the house.

"Sage."

She heaved a huge sigh as they rounded the corner and got out of view of the guests, and, she noted with a quick glance, her father's study window.

"Look, I'm sorry," she said earnestly, lifting her free hand toward the heavens as if to say it wasn't really all her fault. "I really didn't expect you home. Dad said he visited you months ago and you were talking about surfing. So I figured you'd be basking in the sun somewhere, or you know, chasing babes on a beach."

"So you knew I'd be on leave this month?"

"Of course," she said with a shrug, not sure why he sounded so surprised. She always kept track of his schedule. That's how she knew he was safe. "But I didn't think you'd be coming home. If I did, I'd have warned you."

The Spanish tiles, warmed by the sun, were smooth beneath her feet as they crossed onto the lanai. As soon as his boots hit the stone, Aiden pulled his arm from hers and, his frown ferocious, shifted his hands to his hips and gave her the evil eye.

"Warned me? Instead of some drunk slapping me on the back and congratulating me on my score? Or the lady at the grocery store whose name I don't know hugging me and weeping over my upcoming blessing?" He gave a low growl when Sage's lips twitched, so she tried harder to keep the smile from escaping. "Then I get here and instead of a simple explanation, you throw your almost-naked body on me and start a public make-out session?"

"Did you like it?" she asked, as much out of curiosity to feed that tiny seed of hot desire still burning in her belly as to buy some time.

"Why don't you tell me what the hell is going on," he shot back. The stubborn set of his chin and irritation in his gaze told her he'd reached the end of his patience.

Chewing on her bottom lip, she took a deep breath through her teeth. How was she supposed to tell him? Did she ease in with the engagement news, or explain about her father's health first? He wasn't going to take either well.

Before she could decide, she heard the back door open and shut.

Her heart sank toward her bare toes and a now-familiar pain started throbbing in her temple. How was she supposed to handle this? She blinked fast to clear the tears from her eyes, not willing for her father to see her upset. Or to doubt for a single second that his most cherished hope might not come true.

"Please, just go along. I promise, I'll explain everything soon," she whispered, noting her father's footsteps coming closer. "It's for my dad."

Aiden's eyes flicked over her shoulder, then met hers again. He'd only looked away for a millisecond, but she knew from his frown that in that brief glance he'd seen enough to worry him. Good. A worried Aiden was a quiet Aiden. And she needed him to be quiet until she convinced him to go along with her plan.

A plan that'd been so simple when she blurted out that she was in a serious relationship to get Nina and her matchmaking off her back.

One that'd stayed pretty easy when her father, hearing the news, had jumped all over like it was the answer to all of his prayers. After all, how difficult should it be to pretend she and Aiden were engaged? People always expected crazy from her. And Aiden wasn't going to be around.

The ease of her plan had frayed at little at the edges over the last week. The million questions and suggestions about the upcoming fantasy wedding were bad enough. But between trying to process her father's illness and dire prognosis, balanced by his excitement over the news about her and Aiden, she'd been wondering if she'd made a mistake.

And now?

Her plan was looking about as smart as the rocks beneath her feet.

As great as it'd be to hand it all over to Aiden to take care of, Sage knew this scenario had all the makings of a disaster.

Not because it was a crazy idea.

Or that Aiden wouldn't go along.

She sighed, looking at his hard, deliciously muscled body. A body that she was still tingling over plastering herself to. Not listening to a word they said, she watched Aiden greet her father, his soft lips tempting her with every move.

Nope.

It wasn't that the plan was bad, she realized.

It was that she wasn't sure she could resist taking advantage of every single sexual possibility it presented.

3

WHAT THE HELL was going on?

Sage kissed him as though she'd realized he was the answer to her every sexual fantasy, and now she looked as if she was about to fall apart.

While he could handle the kiss—even if that kind of thing was strictly off-limits—the falling apart was a definite cause for concern.

And the Professor looked like... Well, Aiden looked again. He'd rarely thought of the other man as aging. Sure, in the twenty years since they'd first met, there was a little more silver at the temples and the once-robust physique was showing some softening.

But now the old guy appeared to be three steps away from death. Gray-tinged skin seemed to sag from his bones and he looked as though he'd lost twenty pounds and half his hair in the couple of months since Aiden had seen him.

Suddenly feeling as sick as his mentor looked, Aiden's gaze cut to Sage. The quick, tiny shake of her head made it clear she didn't want him to ask questions. He debated. He didn't like waiting, and would definitely prefer to get his information from the Professor. The straight facts, untainted by the emotions emanating from his daughter.

Sage's lips trembled and Aiden sighed. He'd never been able to resist her. Even when he knew better. Even when he had no idea why she drowned herself in the emotional depths she did.

This time was no different.

As if she'd read his mind, and he was never one-hundred-percent sure she couldn't, Sage gave a relieved smile.

"Daddy, would you mind if I stole Aiden away for a little while? We haven't seen each other in so long. I know you need to talk with him, but, well…" The words trailed off as she heaved a sigh deep enough to challenge her bikini top and Aiden's resistance.

Then, either for effect or to try and make his libido explode, she sidled closer, plastered herself against his side and wrapped one arm through his so her breast pressed against his bare bicep.

Aiden bit back a groan. An instant erection over his mentor's daughter while the older man was standing there was poor taste, to say the least.

"I think I should speak with Aiden," the Professor said quietly, not looking any happier about the idea of what he had to share than Aiden knew he was going to be to hear it.

"Daddy, please," Sage said, hitting three syllables on that last word. She threw in a fluttering of her lashes and stopped just short of sticking out her bottom lip. "I know it's important, but can it wait just a little bit?"

His face set in deep furrows, the older man only hesitated for a second before his expression changed from determined to relieved.

"I think I'll take a short nap, then. We'll all meet for dinner?"

He waited for Aiden's nod, then gave them both an indulgent smile before slowly making his way inside.

Sage waited for the door to close before she shifted away. She didn't let go, though. Instead, after a frown at the sliding door her father had gone through, she tugged him around the corner of the house to the French doors, grabbing what looked like a silk towel off the patio chair as they went.

"You know, if your dad had ever been able to resist that big-eyed pleading look, you might not be having to explain what hugely fabricated make-believe story you've dragged me into," Aiden said, letting himself into the family room, crossing the Persian carpet to close the double doors before turning to face her. "Again."

"Again? You say that like I've dragged you into tons of make-believe situations," she protested, shaking out the fabric, then shifting it this way and that until he realized it was a dress and she was looking for the hemline. He wished she'd hurry, since the sooner she found it, the sooner she'd put the damned thing on.

"Shall I make a list? We could start with prom, when you told everyone I was your date so you could get out of going with that football player you didn't like anymore."

"I didn't want to hurt his feelings. Besides, you had fun taking me to prom," she claimed.

Fun? Maybe.

But it'd also been his first introduction to torture, realizing that Sage was everything he found sexy in a woman, and completely off-limits.

Which put that night at the top of his most-regrettable choices list. For a Special Forces officer who'd served multiple missions during wartime, that was saying something.

"Sage." Through playing word games, he wanted information. And his expression made it clear he was going to get it.

"You can be *such* a grump," Sage said, pulling a silky

dress of some sort over her head. He should have been re-lieved when the mossy green fabric covered all that tempt-ing flesh. That he wasn't, he figured, was due to her not giving him his usual buffer time between his typical in-stant lust for her and the point when his well-honed dis-cipline kicked in.

"A grump who's engaged to be married, apparently," Aiden pointed out. Better to take control of the conversa-tion and get right to the point. Otherwise who knew where this discussion would meander.

Despite the worry still etched on her forehead, Sage clapped her hands together and gave him a pleased smile. Why he'd expected her to look ashamed was beyond him.

"Oh, good. You've already heard. That makes breaking the news to you easier."

Aiden tilted his head to one side and shook it a little, wondering if that'd shake his brain cells into the same odd configuration as Sage's apparently were.

"Do you regret nothing, ever?" he asked in wonder.

"Regret? What's to regret?" Suddenly as serious as he'd ever seen her, her face grew ferocious and her eyes fierce. She threw both hands in the air. "My father is dying, Aiden. Hearing that you and I were engaged was like giv-ing him a huge dose of hope. Even his doctor said it's been great for him. Why on earth would I regret that?"

It was like taking a mortar shot to the gut.

Fast, painful and devastating.

For a second, Aiden couldn't breathe. He couldn't think. He couldn't begin to process the immensity of her words, of what they meant.

Clearly not quite the way she'd planned to break it to him, Sage slapped her hand over her mouth, her expres-sion horrified. Then her eyes filled with tears. Before he could decide if he should hug her or run, she held out both hands as if to say *wait*. It only took her a couple of breaths to regain her composure, then she sank onto the couch and gestured that she'd wait until he had processed it all.

How did someone prepare for this kind of hit?

He was trained in war. He was skilled in strategy and stealth ops. He'd learned early into his career with the SEALs to build into every relationship the strong possibility of an abrupt goodbye.

Hell, his career had been founded on loss.

But this?

This was something different.

Suddenly feeling as if his entire world was made up of destruction and death, Aiden pushed his hand through his short-cropped hair and tried to gather his thoughts.

Self-pity and drama wouldn't help anyone, least of all the Professor. And as Sage had already made clear, finding ways to help the older man was their top priority.

"What's the diagnosis?" he asked quietly, finally ready to hear the details.

"Stage three pancreatic," she said hoarsely, watching her fingers twisting the fabric of her dress instead of meeting his eyes. Her way of keeping control of her emotions, he knew.

He needed to research this cancer. See what studies had been done, what treatments were offered. Perhaps there was something experimental they could explore.

But hope and a positive attitude would go further than any treatment, Aiden knew. An oncologist specializing in rare forms of cancer, his own father had shared more than one story about miracle recoveries based on nothing more concrete than optimism and faith.

"Tell me what you've done," he finally said, dropping into a wing-backed chair and gesturing that he was ready to deal with whatever she could dish up.

"It all started when Nina—who just eloped, by the way—tried to fix me up with some guy," Sage began. By the time she'd wound her way around to how her father had heard about their fake engagement at the same time he was telling her the news about his illness, Aiden was shaking his head in awe.

Despite the craziness, it actually all made perfect sense. Well, Sage sense, which was usually perfect in hindsight.

"So that's how we ended up engaged," she said with a deep sigh. "I've tried to find a way to wriggle out of it, but you're so great in my father's eyes that nothing I've said will convince him that you aren't perfect. For me, even."

"For you, even," he repeated, laughing helplessly and admiring Sage's easy acceptance of her own flaws. "Now that's saying something."

"It's making him happy," she said, looking down at her tangled fingers and giving a sigh heavy enough to break a heart. "It's giving him hope and a purpose. I cringe every time he mentions the wedding, but he glows. How can this be a mistake if it helps him get better?"

How, indeed.

"What if he expects an actual ceremony?"

She was shaking her head before he finished the words.

"He knows I won't get married while worrying about his health. That'd be bad juju."

Aiden's grimace quickly shifted to a rueful grin. Looked like all that new-agey stuff she was obsessed over might pay off.

"And the exit plan?" he asked. Never commit to a mission without a clear way out.

"When he's better, and cleared by at least two doctors, we realize that we aren't suited. I'm thinking we blame your career choice," she said, batting her eyelashes and giving him a look so sexy and persuasive that he was nodding before he realized what she'd said.

"What? Why my career?"

"Because I don't have one." For a second, her lower lip poked out in a cute pout. "And before you suggest we blame it on me being too flighty, I've always been that way. He's not going to believe you changed your mind over something that's always been a fact."

It took Aiden a second or two to follow that logic, but once he did, he had to admit she was right.

"Okay, fine," he said grudgingly. "We can blame my commitment to being a SEAL. Statistics will support that claim."

Hopefully a few of his team would beat the odds, since two were recently married and one newly engaged. But military and marriage weren't a good bet under most odds. Factor in the added issues of Special Forces, with the extra dangers and secrecy, and the odds got a little longer.

"Ahhh, statistics," Sage said fondly. Then she rolled her eyes. "A nice fallback and one my father will undoubtedly let himself believe. But we all know that I'm not statistically correct."

"Are you any kind of correct?" Aiden asked in exasperation.

She pondered for a moment, her fingernail tapping on her lower lip in a way that made his mouth water.

"I'm sexually correct."

"You do sex correctly?" he clarified before he could stop himself.

"Oh, God, no," she said, laughing. "How boring would that be? I'm sexually correct in that I'm the perfect sexual orientation for all of my sexual preferences."

Aiden had to sigh.

It was that, or drop his head into his hands and groan.

What was it about Sage that let her take a completely crazy statement, twist it into knots so it made perfect sense, and turn him on all at the same time?

He'd always found smart women sexy.

And Sage, God help them both, was brilliant. Twisted, flighty and very out there. But, his body insisted as it hardened in appreciation, definitely brilliant.

SAGE BIT HER LIP, trying not to laugh aloud at the frustrated expression on Aiden's face. She'd never in a million years have allowed her imagination to venture into a scenario that had her father fighting for his life, and his battle dependent on she and Aiden pretending to be in love.

But since they were there, she was starting to think this might actually be kinda fun. Or at least, fun enough playing with Aiden to distract her from the terror dogging her every thought.

"Okay," he said, waving his hand as if trying to erase all of her crazy comments. "Time to get serious."

"Ahh, then you're taking charge now," she murmured.

He shot her a look that said she was stepping outside the serious line, and had better behave. Sage was tempted to ask if he'd spank her if she didn't.

But she was afraid she might like his answer a little too much.

"If this is going to work we have to see it as a mission," Aiden said, his words clipped and his tone cool. Official, she realized, leaning forward and clasping her hands together in anticipation. She'd never seen Aiden in military mode. This should be fun.

"Are you listening?" he asked, giving her a narrow look, his dark eyes assessing her seriousness.

As tempting as it was to tease him, Sage managed to keep her expression sincere. After all, she wanted this to work more than anything. Well, except for seeing him take command. That, she was *really* looking forward to.

"Of course I'm listening," she said, gesturing with a finger wave that he keep it coming. "We're on a mission. Of course, I've never been on a mission before. Unless you count those two months I belonged to the Commune of the Sacred Light up in Seattle and tried to convert the pescatarians to pork. You know, the other white meat."

"I thought chicken—" Aiden cut himself off with a shake of his head, then gave her a chiding look. "Do you want us to successfully pull off this fake engagement or not? Either you call the shots, or I do."

The tight knot that'd tangled her heart and guts so miserably the last week loosened for the first time. Not just because Aiden was home and taking charge. But because finally, here was someone who could actually distract her enough to keep from worrying every single second.

Diving into the distraction, she debated suggesting they share the shots, preferably out of a tequila bottle. But she figured that'd go over about as well as the pork idea had. Although Aiden probably wouldn't threaten to roast her over a barbecue like the gang at the commune had. Who knew living on just seafood could make hemp-wearers so bloodthirsty.

"Call away," she instructed, waving one hand regally as she leaned back on the couch and got comfy. Better him than her. She wasn't so good at the making-rules thing. Mostly because she never cared about following them. But rules and Aiden? Peanut butter and jelly.

Something he was clearly aware of, since rather than looking surprised, he instead gave a nod to indicate he'd expected nothing less. Mulling with his chin low, he got up from the chair. He paced two steps to the right, clasped his hands behind his back like a general plotting a coup, paced two steps to the left, then faced her again.

"Okay, then, here we go. The obvious goal of the mission is to offer peace of mind to the Professor." He waited for Sage to agree, which she quickly did, then gave an answering nod. "Which, to him, is the concept of both of us being settled and happy. Marriage, as he's hinted at from time to time over the last decade, is his ultimate goal."

Say what? Her father had dropped plenty of hints to her over the years. Hints she'd laughed at. But he'd tossed a few at Aiden, too? To the same reaction? She frowned. It was one thing for her to think they were totally unsuitable and the idea of them as a couple was funny. But she was oddly insulted that Aiden felt the same.

Then it hit her that this mission, as Aiden was calling it, was something her father really, really wanted. It was so important to him, and it might be the last thing he ever asked of her.

Suddenly all of the other things he'd ever asked bombarded her. That she come home for Christmas. That she get a degree. The three weeks he'd spent nagging her to see a dentist to make sure her tongue piercing wasn't going to ruin her teeth. The concern he'd shown over the guy she was dating. Any guy, she realized. He'd been concerned about them all. To the point that, somewhere after her twentieth birthday, she'd stopped letting him meet them. All because it'd been easier than worrying about making her father happy.

What did that say about her? And how much longer did she have to worry about his happiness? Her chest too tight to pull in a deep breath, Sage bit her lip and tried to keep from crying.

"Sage?"

She took a shallow breath, trying to get air to her lungs.

The pain was too much, though. She debated putting her head between her knees. But while she wasn't averse to a head between her knees, she didn't want it to be her own. Nor did she want to explain why it was there to Aiden.

Because that'd be admitting fear. Admitting that she didn't believe that smiles and positive energy and this crazy scheme were going to be enough to pull her father through.

"Sage?" Aiden asked again, stepping over to lean down and peer at her face.

"I'm okay," she croaked.

"What's wrong?"

Unable—unwilling—to explain, she shrugged and waved at Aiden to keep barking out rules.

He narrowed his eyes, stepping closer as if he were going to offer comfort. Then, since he probably didn't figure mission leaders were supposed to hand out hugs, he frowned instead and gave her a nod.

"If we're going to succeed, we both have to be completely committed to whatever means necessary to fulfill said mission."

Blinking back the tears that were burning her eyelids, Sage sniffed and forced herself to focus on Aiden instead of her morbid thoughts.

A good choice, since he made for a great view. He was so cute, all serious and intense. Unable to resist, Sage widened her eyes and asked, "Will that include night-vision goggles, matching camo outfits and secret passwords?"

"Maybe," he said without even a hint of a smile. "But more to the point is that we both agree that we'll give this one hundred percent. If you want the Professor's mind at ease, it's going to take focus and effort."

Sage frowned. Neither of which he seemed to think she had. Needing a few seconds to process that, she leaned back, tucking her feet under her. The nubby fabric of the sofa scraped gently over her bare toes, contrasting with the silk of her skirt.

"This isn't a whim, Aiden. This isn't an experiment or a fun lark. This is my father." She paused, as much to swallow the tight ball of fear in her throat as for effect. "I'll do whatever it takes, for as long as it takes, to bring him comfort and to keep him from worrying. So if Mission Marriage is the answer to his peace of mind, consider me in."

He gave her a look so intense and searching, she felt like he'd just scanned her every thought, delved into her secrets and checked her pockets for loose change.

If he could package that, TSA would pay a fortune.

Sage shifted, angling her feet under her butt to keep herself from getting up to run from that look. Or, more to the point, from discovering what he'd found. Or worse, what he hadn't.

As usual, he didn't say.

Instead, he shook his head, then instructed, "Let's call it Mission Engagement. Neither of us is crazy enough to think we're marriage material."

Sage blinked a couple of times, trying to process that kick in the gut. She wasn't marriage material? As in, he didn't think she was marriageable? Or was she simply not what he wanted in marriage?

Not sure why she cared, since marriage—especially marriage to someone like Aiden—was the last thing *she* wanted, Sage frowned.

Whether it was intuition, that he caught the look on her face or he was just in a hurry, Aiden waved his hand as if turning the page. Then he followed it up with lifting two fingers in the air.

"Point one is that this is a mission. Which means point two is that we agree that to better ensure the success of the mission, the truth of the situation would be kept between just the two of us. Under no circumstances is anyone else to know that this is a fake engagement."

"So you wouldn't actually want to marry me, but you don't want anyone to think you'd fake our engagement?" she clarified.

"I didn't say I wouldn't want to marry you," he corrected, pushing his hands into the front pockets of his jeans. His brow furrowed, a frustrated look in his eyes as he shrugged. "But wanting something doesn't mean you should do it. That's kindergarten one-oh-one."

"I must have napped through that lesson." Her own more casual shrug shifted the loose fabric of her dress so it slid down one shoulder.

Something flashed in his eyes as his gaze followed the silk's slide. Something hot and wild and edgy enough to make Sage's nerves tighten and heat swirl low in her belly. Then he blinked and the look was gone, leaving Sage wondering if celibacy was causing her to hallucinate.

The hot warmth between her thighs and the delicious tightening of her nipples weren't just her imagination, though.

"So marrying me wouldn't be so bad?" she teased, her words low and husky, a hint of flirty enticement in her smile.

"Of course it would."

Huh?

"You said…" The words trailed off as she shook her head. Debating her many failings in his eyes wasn't going to help them comfort her father. "Forget it. You were outlining the mission rules. Go ahead."

"Okay," he said, his gaze narrowed as if he were checking something off his mental list. He gave a short nod before continuing. "Rule three, the mission time frame is completely dependent on the health of the Professor. The mission is not complete until his health is completely recovered, or, well, until it's no longer necessary."

Nausea swam through Sage's belly at his hesitation. Unwilling to acknowledge it, she tilted her head to the side, focusing instead on the way his shirt emphasized his biceps. Tight, hard round muscles that made her mouth water. That, she decided, was a much more enticing focal point.

"That means we're both fully committed, Sage," he said, his tone making it clear he didn't think she was hearing him. Since he might have already recited the Gettysburg Address for all she knew, he had a good point.

"Fine, yes," she agreed quickly. "We're fully committed."

"This might not be accomplished in one leave, or this month. Or even this year. I have to go back on duty, and you're going to be, well, wherever you're going to be."

"Here," she decided then and there. "I'm here until my dad is well again."

"All the more reason to make sure you're following rule three then."

"Fully committed?"

"That means you're pretending you're engaged." He paused, giving her an arch look. She was pretty sure she knew where he was going, but decided it would be more fun to make him spell it out. So she offered a blank look of confusion, adding a flutter of her lashes for good measure.

"I know this is going to be hard for you, but unless you can handle it, we might as well find an alternative now."

Not so amused any longer, she ceased fluttering.

"Handle...what?" Hard and handling were giving her a lot of ideas.

"You have to be able to commit to keeping to the spirit

of this engagement for the duration. That means no sex. You can't keep bouncing from guy to guy."

Bouncing? Sage was tempted to inform him that she was going on eight months with no sex and managing fine. But that wasn't the kind of thing a girl wanted to admit to a guy who was currently making her wonder how many licks of his tongue it would take to get her off.

At least, not until they'd spent a little more time together, and she'd figured out what it was about Aiden that was suddenly making her hot and crazy.

"I promise, any sex I have will be within the accepted confines of our engagement," she swore, one hand in the air.

"That'd be rule four," he said quickly. "No sex."

"I just said I wasn't going to cheat on you. Even if the cheating was really fake."

"I mean no sex between us."

Sage was sure her jaw hit her chest so hard it bounced back.

"I beg your pardon?" He was kidding, wasn't he?

Except he didn't look like he was kidding. He had that serious, man-in-charge, military face on again.

"Sage, as tempting as it might be to get carried away by the pretense, we aren't actually engaged. So no sex." He said it so adamantly she had to wonder which one of them he was bossing around. "And no situations that might lead to sex. No scenarios that might give each other an idea to create a situation that might lead to sex."

That's it. She'd had enough.

He was only doing this for her father.

She got that.

He didn't see her as marriage material, because wanting something didn't mean you should have it. Whatever that meant.

Fine.

But if he thought he got to call the shots when it came to her and sex, he was sadly out of his mind.

Because Sage Taylor had a policy against letting any man tell her how, where or when she'd enjoy sexual pleasures.

Aiden had just offered up a tidy lesson on the merits of mission planning and strategy.

Now it was his turn to learn a thing or two.

Call it her way of saying thank-you.

Not sure what she was going to do, only knowing she was going to make damned sure they both enjoyed it, Sage slowly lowered her feet to the floor.

The move sent her skirt floating, sliding along her bare limbs like liquid. Aiden's hazel eyes followed the fabric, settling for a long second on her bare toes before he yanked his gaze back to meet hers.

Sage smiled.

A slow, seductive smile.

Then in a sinuous move she'd learned from the belly dancers in Persia, she got to her feet, her fingers skimming her hips, up her waist before she teased them along the sides of her breasts and up to her throat.

Wetting her lips, she gave a deep sigh. Aiden's gaze dropped to her breasts and his own lips tightened. If the fit of his jeans were anything to go by, something else was getting tight, too. He didn't look too happy about that. But Sage's goal was horny, not happy.

She stepped closer.

From the wild look in his eyes, she figured it was a credit to his SEAL training that he didn't step back. Because he clearly didn't want her body this tight against his. Or, he didn't *want* to want her this close.

"You go ahead and set those rules," she told him quietly, tapping one finger against his chest, then against his chin.

"You saying you won't follow them?"

"Rules one through three? I'm one-hundred percent committed."

He closed his eyes for just a second, then gave her an arch look.

"And rule four?"

"Babe, enforcing that one is all on you." She gave one last tap, this one on the tempting fullness of his lower lip. Then, for good measure, she leaned close and brushed her own lips over that same spot before giving him a wide smile. "Good luck with that."

4

AIDEN HAD A HANGOVER.

Not the partying-all-night, drinking-too-much-booze kind of hangover, though.

Nope, this was a sex hangover.

The kind that came from being up all night—in every meaning of the term—obsessing over the sex he wasn't having. Not the random, with-any-woman, getting-laid-felt-good kind of sex, though.

Nope. He'd been obsessing about sex with Sage.

Sex under the swimming pool's waterfall at midnight.

Sex in the gazebo at the bottom of the hill at noon.

Sex on his bed. Sex on her bed. Sex in various hotel beds.

Missionary sex. Doggy-style sex. Up-against-the-wall sex. Sweet and reverent sex. Pornworthy sex.

Hell, by dawn, he'd been imagining the kinds of sex he'd barely been aware existed before.

Damn Sage.

And damn her daring him to enforce rule four.

He threw his car into gear, heading up the hill toward the Taylor house. He hadn't seen his so-called fiancée since she'd offered a vague excuse of rejoining her friends, leaving Aiden and the Professor to have dinner alone together the previous night.

Just as well. He'd had enough trouble hearing the details of the Professor's health issues—officially—from the Professor. Aiden knew it would have been even harder for Sage to hear it again. Especially as the Professor had taken the intellectual route, detailing the various options, side effects and prognosis statistics.

You'd have thought that information, the dire possibilities, would have filled Aiden's head all night instead of the vivid fantasies of doing his mentor's daughter.

Before he could sink into yet another one of those fantasies, his cell phone buzzed. Normally he'd ignore it. But desperate for a distraction, he pulled to the side of the road and hit talk.

"Dude, you on a beach covered in half-naked chicks yet?"

Aiden smirked. Leave it to Castillo to get right to the point.

"Nope. No beach, no naked chicks. What's up?"

"Big mission."

Aiden rolled his eyes. Castillo was as long-winded as he was subtle.

"I'm on leave."

"You don't wanna miss this one."

That's all the lieutenant said. Not because he was trying to be sly, but because protocol mandated that anything about the mission was classified. Even though Aiden was a part of the team, he wasn't on duty, this wasn't a secure line and he hadn't been briefed by a commanding officer.

"No can do. I came home to some rough news."

Castillo was silent for a second before clearing his throat and offering a rough, "Sucks, man."

Despite the pounding in his temples and the stress of

the situation, Aiden had to grin. The guy should be writing Hallmark cards.

"Without you, Banks is going to pull recon duty," Castillo pointed out. "Last mission we did with him, he hot-dogged the whole thing."

"He's good at his job," Aiden pointed out fairly.

Still, he knew how Castillo felt. Banks had joined the team late last year, a replacement for Carter.

The sudden pain, the reminder of losing his buddy on that mission last winter, hit Aiden like a kick in the gut. Intellectually, he knew that was the risk they all took. Not just by putting their lives on the line, but by caring about the other guys who were right there with them. But for once, Aiden didn't find any comfort in logic.

Still, that's the way the military was. Nobody was irreplaceable. Even as specially trained and elite as the SEALs were, when one fell, another was there to step into his place.

Most days, Aiden accepted that as fact.

These days, it was just another fingernail on his emotional chalkboard.

"Don't like working with divas," Castillo grunted, pulling Aiden's attention back to the phone call. The lieutenant was a guy who believed the old adage, there's no I in Team.

"He's good at what he does," Aiden repeated. "He's got solid recon training, and he's a damned good medic."

"Just because he's got skills doesn't mean he's got heart," Castillo said.

Heart was everything.

That's what made a team, well, a team.

Aiden had only served one mission with Banks, but from what he'd observed so far, Castillo was right. The guy was a loner. That didn't mean he didn't have heart, though. Hell, Aiden was an integral part of the team and he wasn't sure of his own heart anymore.

It was either gone or buried.

Dammit.

"I'll call you in five," he said, hitting the off button before he could give in to temptation and say more.

Aiden stared, unseeing, out the windshield, row after row of grapevines a blur.

Was he burned out? Was he just overwhelmed by the emotional impact of losing Carter, of facing the very real possibility of losing Professor Taylor?

Or was his brain blood-starved after an exhausted night of horny overload?

Aiden considered all of those valid reasons for his current stress level, and none of them necessary reasons for him to head back early. He was a dedicated SEAL, his entire life revolving around serving his country.

A few people, especially here in Villa Rosa, thought he served for revenge. That he'd joined the navy with a laser focus on being a SEAL because of his parents' death in the Twin Towers attack.

Those people were wrong.

And they were right.

He had joined with the goal of stopping terrorists. But not for revenge. Intellectually, revenge wasn't strategic. But actively working to prevent that kind of thing from ever happening again? There was enough strategy in that for Aiden to be comfortable making it a career. A calling, even.

He sighed. Glanced at his phone.

Would he be heading back because it was his calling? Because he was necessary for the success of this mission?

Nope.

As good as he was, he was just another tool in the

SEALs' arsenal. A damned good one, but he wasn't irreplaceable.

Bottom line, he wanted to escape.

He just wasn't sure what he was trying to escape from.

He actually wanted to turn the car around, head straight for the airport and leave a message at the Taylors' that he'd been called back on duty.

They'd both unquestionably accept his decision. While neither understood his career choice, they'd never questioned his devotion to it either.

It was the perfect excuse. Then he could lose himself in a mission that would demand one-hundred-and-ten percent of his focus. He could put all worries of the Professor's health out of his mind. And he could avoid any and all physical contact with Sage. The more he was with her, the hotter the fantasies were getting. But this mission would mean he'd most likely be halfway around the world, being shot at. It was pretty damned difficult to entertain sexual fantasies while dodging bullets.

He rested his forehead on the steering wheel, hating the decision he knew he was about to make.

Hating the drama it was going to embroil him in and the slew of tangled, messy problems it was guaranteed to create.

But hating a situation had never stopped him from facing it before. So he reached for his phone.

"No can do," he told Castillo when the other guy answered. "I've got my own life-or-death scenario here, complete with its own set of hazards and challenges."

IT WAS ABOUT TIME.

Sage had been watching for Aiden all morning. Peeking through the front curtains like a nosy neighbor, or worse, a lovesick schoolgirl, for the past hour. Finally, he was here.

Her eyes narrowed as she peered through the window. He looked terrible.

She wasn't sure if it was worry over her father that had him looking so unhappy. Or if he was feeling the misery of their engagement. Preferably the latter, since she could charm him out of that. Hopefully.

"Good morning," Sage greeted in a singsong tone, welcoming him with a bright smile as he mounted the front steps. Sunshine filled the porch, haloing around his head, adding intensity to his furrowed brow and grumpy look. All those years in the military didn't seem to have made Aiden a morning person.

No matter. Sage loved mornings enough for both of them. So much so that she widened her smile and shifted to gesture him inside. As soon as he crossed the threshold, she stood on tiptoe to brush a kiss across his cheek. Then pressed her lips tight together to keep from grinning at his scowl.

Yep. He was still a morning grump.

A cute one, too, she noted, her smile dimming.

"You're just in time," she said, determined to ignore the sexual flutter in her tummy as the scent of his soap wrapped around her. "We need to talk over plans for our engagement party before my dad wakes up from his nap."

"An engagement party?" Aiden looked horrified as he handed her the white sack filled with delicious scents.

Sage's stomach growled and her mouth watered.

She spent most of her life focusing on being healthy. Spirit, mind and body, she fed them all the best.

Daily meditation, thought-provoking books. And a healthy organic diet. Whole foods, low fats and lots of vegetables.

She didn't pollute her spirit with nastiness, her mind with negativity. Or her body with processed foods.

But Tilly's donuts were special.

Amazingly special.

She sniffed the rich cinnamon-filled air, all but licking her lips. Of course, Tilly's apple-cinnamon donuts went beyond amazingly simple into the realms of magic.

And Sage made a point to always embrace magic.

She'd like to embrace it right here in the foyer, but she had the feeling that Mrs. Green, her father's housekeeper, would smack her if she did.

"What do you mean, we're having an engagement party?" Aiden prodded, not caring that she was contemplating magic. "That's a stupid idea."

Hmm. She peered at his face, noting that he looked more irritated than upset. A night's sleep at his own place and a delicious breakfast at Tilly's clearly hadn't gotten him any closer to embracing their newfound coupledom. Sage gave him a long look, noting that he didn't look any more rested this morning than he had after traveling yesterday.

Jet lag over flying home from who knew where?

Or something deeper?

She tilted her head to one side, her hair sliding in a heavy wave over her bare shoulder to tickle her elbow. Aiden never talked about the navy. When he was home, it was as if that part of his life was a completely different world. Here, he was supergeek, the cute brainiac who cozied up with the Professor to feed his brain cells.

But this time he didn't seem to be shaking off the stress. Granted, it wasn't yet even twenty-four hours since he'd crossed the city limits. Nor had Sage been home at the same time he was in over two years. So maybe this was SOP for Chief Petty Officer Masters.

But she was still worried.

"Earth to Sage," he said, looking irritated when she

frowned. "We were having a conversation. You want to rejoin it?"

"No. You were offering your opinion of the intelligence of having an engagement party," she corrected precisely. Since asking was pointless, Sage decided to keep a close eye on him until she was sure Aiden wasn't hurting over something more than her father's prognosis. Stress, she knew he could deal with. Worry was part and parcel of his personality. But if he was hurting, she'd have to step in and help. Somehow.

"It is a stupid idea. Why the hell would we want to have one?" No longer just looking exhausted, he'd added horrified to his expression. Sage didn't know if the reaction was specific to their situation, or if almost any guy would be just as freaked at being told he was going on groom-grooming display.

"Because my father has decided he wants to throw one, that's why," she told him with a sniff. "Besides, you say that like I just told you we were being invaded by a marauding band of pygmies."

"Do pygmies maraud in bands? Actually that might be interesting to see," he said thoughtfully. "Did you know that some groups of pygmies were hunted by cannibals? With that kind of incentive, I'll bet they've learned to maraud pretty well."

"No, no. No pygmy lessons," Sage protested quickly, waving both hands in the air as she rolled her eyes. "Instead, tell me what you'd find more threatening than interesting."

"A biochemical attack by terrorists?"

She shuddered, giving him a horrified look.

"What?" he asked with a shrug. "That's a threat."

"You put our engagement party in the same category

as a biochemical terrorist attack?" She wasn't sure if she should laugh, or smack him.

"Fake engagement party. And the subtle and overt dangers of both are cause for concern," he told her, his tone deadly serious.

That hurt. It actually hurt. Her lower lip trembled. It took a second, then Sage saw a glint in his eyes. A little of the tension that'd been creeping into knots along her shoulders faded and she blew out a relieved breath.

"You worry me sometimes," she told him, shaking her head.

"Ditto."

"Me?" Truly shocked, Sage pressed her palm against her chest and gave him an openmouthed look of surprise. "What do I do that's worrisome?"

Unlike some people who regularly jumped out of perfectly good airplanes to go into battles and be shot at, she was the epitome of mellow.

"Let's see. You traipsed off to Tibet with a guy named Moon Petal. You sold your car and donated the money to a research group attempting to teach dogs to talk. When you volunteered at that recovery program in Brooklyn, a heroin junkie tried to use you to mop the floor because he didn't like your views on using happy thoughts to overcome the shakes." He paused, for a breath, she realized, not to try and think up more examples.

"Aww, you read my blog," she realized, her heart warming at the news. He just scowled, then slanted his head to the side as if reminding her to get back on track.

"Okay, fine," she said. "So I've been cause for a little worry in the past. That has nothing to do with right now."

"You're trying to rope me into a fake party."

"And you hate parties," she remembered with a grimace. "Who needs a bunch of strangers around demanding attention and forcing you to engage in social chitchat? I'd rather hang out with a few people I actually like."

"There will be a few people you actually like there," she vowed, clueless where she'd find them. "I promise."

He huffed, then shrugged as if giving in.

"Besides, this isn't a fake party," she reminded him. "You're the one who said we have to treat Mission Engagement as if it's real. So it stands to reason that people—and by people, I mean my father—would want to throw us a party, a real one, to celebrate."

"It's not a good idea," he argued. Whether out of simple stubbornness or because he really did foresee huge pitfalls, she wasn't sure. "There's a lot that could go wrong."

"Don't be such a worrywart," she said, laughing. "It's only a party. No big deal."

The look Aiden gave her was exasperated, frustrated and just a bit baffled. In other words, the same look he'd been giving her most of their lives.

"Tell you what. We'll spend an afternoon, a couple of evenings together. We'll go over every possible scenario, map out all of those scary pitfalls you're so worried about. We'll get to know each other so well that we could win one of those newlywed games."

"I hate games," he muttered.

"I love them."

"Shock."

Sage laughed, delighted in his dry humor and exasperated look. He was so sweet. Why hadn't she realized that before? Or had she, and just ignored it because of his relationship with her father?

The smart thing to do would be to keep this all friendly and sweet. Nothing naughty that'd get them into trouble. But...she liked naughty. Especially when naughty provided such a wonderful distraction to worrying about her father, about her future.

Unable to resist, she stepped closer. It was what she imagined getting close to a lightning bolt would feel like. Electric energy zapped through her system, making her feel edgy and needy and excited. And, at the same time, a little nervous.

Like, who knew what could happen if she reached out.

If she touched.

If she tasted.

Excitement stirred, needy and intense, deep in her belly. Her eyes met Aiden's. The look in his hazel gaze should have warned her to be careful. Maybe tipped her off that she was about to get into a whole lot of trouble if she didn't take a very careful step backward.

Her heart thumped faster. And, like everything else she'd ever encountered that offered the possibility of delight and bliss, she couldn't resist.

She had to see how it felt. How he felt.

She pressed her hands against his chest, her hands flat to better explore the delicious expanse of muscles under his shirt. *Oh, my, they built them hard in the navy.* So deliciously hard.

She wet her lips, then gave a low husky sigh of appreciation.

"Sage..." Aiden warned.

But he didn't move.

So she did.

Closer. She slid her hands over his shoulders, her fingers tickling the back of his neck. He gave a slow shake of his head. She took that as a sign to move faster, before he sped up the denial.

So move she did. Her lips brushed his. First a soft caress. Just a sweet hello from her mouth to his.

His body tensed. She'd like to think it was passion, but more likely he was going to push her away.

So she stepped up her game. And pressed her body closer. The tips of her breasts grazed his chest. She almost moaned as desire swirled from her quickly hardening nipples to her belly. Her thighs felt heavy, loose. Her breathing grew deeper and the blood slowed as if everything in her body were preparing for how great this was going to feel.

Always willing to give her body what it wanted, she curled her fingers tighter around the back of Aiden's neck. She slid her tongue along the crease of his lips, tasting.

Testing.

He tasted damned good.

For a second, she thought he was going to just stand there. Stoic and sweet, simply tolerating the move but not rejecting her so as not to hurt her feelings.

Then he gave a low growl.

The sound sent those tingles into high gear. Sage's heart sped up. His mouth opened over hers.

Hot and swift, his tongue swept in. Took over.

This was a man used to command.

Sage liked it.

His lips molded, his tongue thrust.

Her body melted.

Then, slowly, as if not wanting to send her system into instant withdrawal, he slowed it down.

He changed the kiss, so just his lips were sweeping over hers. His fingers loosened. His body shifted, just a little, as if inviting air in to cool things off between them.

Whew.

Talk about acing the test.

"Well," she breathed slowly. "That was fun."

Sage had to step away from that delicious body in order to get her body's circuits to connect to her brain again.

She felt as if everything had gone haywire, all her systems sparking and zinging with passion unlike anything she'd ever experienced.

Something to think about, she promised herself. Later. Much later. After she'd had a few hours away from Aiden and a lot of meditation to neutralize her reaction.

"You play with live grenades for fun, too?" he asked quietly, his expression neutral, with a hint of something intense, something ferocious beneath the surface.

She wanted to touch again. To see what that passion felt like. What he'd do with it. How he'd use it on her body. She shivered at the prospect, then carefully took one more step away from temptation.

Not out of fear, she promised herself.

Just good judgment.

Something she liked to try out every once in a while for a change of pace.

"That was a thanks for the donut." Sage laughed again, and delicious bag-o-magic swinging in her hand, made her way to the kitchen. Leaving the grumpy pessimist to find her father on his own.

TWO HOURS LATER, she wasn't quite as amused.

Seated by the swimming pool, an umbrella shading them from the afternoon sun, two of her best friends were plotting to drive her crazy.

"Look, it's really not a big deal," she told them, trying to sound cheerful and calm instead of panicked and worried. "Let's talk about something else. Like Nina's eloping."

"Not a big deal? Are you kidding, this is huge," Cailley protested, ignoring the subject change and spreading her hands apart in the classic indicator usually saved for detailing guy parts. "A term I hear applies to more than just the situation. I hear rumors about your fiancé that are pretty impressive, if you know what I mean."

Even Sage had to giggle at that.

Aiden was going to so gloat when he heard.

Not that Cailley thought he was huge.

But that her friends were trying to make a big deal of the party. Of the entire engagement, actually.

Still, as fun as it was going to be to tell him that the general opinion was that he was hung, and as hard as it'd be to admit that he was right about this party getting out of hand, those things weren't what was bothering Sage.

For the first time, she wished her friends weren't around. Wished they didn't care about the excitement and fun that was her life. Or, in this case, her make-believe life.

"I want more details," Nina insisted. "Where is your ring? What does it look like?"

"The ring?" Uh oh. She hadn't even thought about a ring. "We're still looking for just the right one."

"That's important," Nina allowed. Then she leaned forward. "So how did he propose? When did the two of you start spending time together? Last I heard, you were miserable in Arizona and he was off, you know, somewhere doing whatever."

She waved her hand over her head to indicate that vague *wherever* that Aiden did his navy thing at.

"It's really not that exciting," Sage murmured, focusing all of her attention on sucking iced tea through her straw instead of meeting her friends' eyes. Who knew Aiden's no-telling rule would be so painful.

Her gaze flicked toward the house. She couldn't see her father from here, but his study window was open, the curtains fluttering in the breeze. He liked working to fresh air. The immediate weight of miserable worry wrapped over her, making any discomfort over the fake engagement instantly bearable.

"C'mon, Sage," Nina said as she nibbled on a handful of M&M's from the table between them. "We've been sharing the details of our love lives since we were too young to have them."

"Nina's right. And you always have the best details," Cailley said with a laugh. "Besides, this is Aiden. Which means it's like, doubly juicy details."

Sage laughed. She leaned forward, ready to share just how juicy Aiden kissed. Now there was a detail worth reliving.

Then she stopped.

As soon as she shared the kiss story, they'd want more. And there was no way they'd believe that Sage and Aiden hadn't done more. As Cailley said, the guy was known for being hung, and Sage was known for being curious.

She shot a narrow-eyed look toward the house again. It wasn't as if Aiden would hear if she told them. And they were her best friends. They'd keep the secret.

Sage tossed back a handful of M&M's. They were the only unhealthy treat she allowed herself—besides Tilly's donuts—and she was trying to find comfort in their crunchy-coated chocolaty goodness.

But…Sage didn't break promises, and she'd agreed to keep it just between her and Aiden. Besides, this was her father's health and happiness at stake.

"There's something you're not telling us," Nina accused, her eyes narrowed. She leaned forward, pulling the candy dish away from Sage. "You just ate those M&M's without sorting the colors. What's going on?"

Wide-eyed, Sage looked at her friend, then at the candy in her fist. Hell. Nina was right. Sage never mixed colors when she ate her M&M's.

"Nothing's going on," she lied. She tried a flutter of her lashes and a deep sigh. "I was just thinking about Aiden and got distracted."

"Right," Cailley said slowly, her expression just as suspicious as Nina's. "You know, if you don't tell us what's going on, we won't tell you about the engagement party plans."

The look she and Nina shared was two shades past naughty, hinting at wicked.

"My father is putting the party on," Sage said slowly. What could be naughty about that? Her father's idea of wild was 10:00 p.m., a second glass of wine while listening to his Elvis vinyls. "I'm sure it's going to be a fun—if a little mellow—evening."

"You've missed the last couple of engagement parties, haven't you?" Nina asked with a laugh that didn't bode well for any plans Aiden had to keep things chill between them.

Eyes wide, Cailley opened her mouth as if to say something, but took a deep breath and offered a big smile instead.

"What's going on?" she asked, leaning forward in both worry and anticipation. Because, well, naughty was usually fun. "What happened at the last couple of engagement parties?"

"Nothing you need to worry about. We've got to go, though," Nina said, wrapping her hand around Cailley's forearm and pulling the other woman to her feet. "We'll talk to you later, okay? Let your dad know we'll be happy to help out."

If Sage hadn't been worried already, the look on Nina's face would have done the trick.

"What are you helping with, exactly?" she asked narrowly.

"Just helping. You know, with food and entertainment

and stuff," Cailley added, her grin so wide she looked like a Halloween decoration. "I'll call him tomorrow. Could you let him know?"

"I don't think he needs a lot of help," Sage said quickly, getting to her feet, too. "He'll cater a dinner, throw on a few CDs and make a toast. Simple and easy."

"I'll call him," Cailley said again.

Before Sage could protest, they were gone.

She debated following them and nagging for information.

But she wasn't the following, nor the nagging type.

She might have to learn to be the apologizing type if whatever they had planned upset Aiden. But she'd deal with that when the time came.

Besides, she grinned, she was kinda looking forward to finding out what'd put that wicked gleam in their eyes.

It was the kind of gleam that boded naughty for their intended target. "Sage?"

Ahh, her fellow target.

Still smiling, Sage turned toward the house and Aiden's call.

It wasn't like she was really horny for Aiden.

She was just enjoying the game.

And she'd keep telling herself that until she'd decided how she felt about it, either way.

5

"Why are you doing this again?" Aiden asked, watching Sage putter around his kitchen, her hair tied back and an oddly peaceful look on her face.

"I told you. We need to spend some time together. To get to know each other again well enough that people will buy our story." Pulling the oven door open, she bent low, giving Aiden a tasty view of her butt as the filmy fabric of her skirt pulled tight.

His mouth dirt-dry, he took a swig of beer, swished it, then took another drink for good measure.

"Besides," she said, straightening and turning to face him. Worry lines creased her brow and her pale eyes held a hint of confusion. "We need to get all the engagement details right."

Since she'd been awfully mellow about pulling this off when she'd kissed him stupid that morning, Aiden had to surmise that something had gone down between then and now.

He considered his bottled brew with a sigh.

"Why don't you fill me in?" he suggested, settling into the ladder-back chair and pulling the bowl of chips and guacamole Sage had set out closer. He had the feeling he was going to need sustenance.

"Shouldn't we decide the engagement details together? Agree on why I don't have a ring. Or you know, each of us share our favorite scenario, then we'll see if they can somehow mesh together? That way we're more likely to remember it."

A chip loaded with creamy avocado and jalapeno, Aiden squinted at her.

"You think I have an engagement scenario? One that has nothing to do with enemy combat?"

She blinked a couple of times, then rolled her eyes as she put the terms *enemy engagement* together in her head.

"Fine, so you don't lie awake at night in your cot dreaming of your perfect woman and the most romantic way to invite her to spend your lives together."

Aiden's gaze softened as he crunched his chip. He was usually so exasperated with Sage that he forgot how sweet she was. Since any nights he lay awake in his cot thinking about a woman usually involved her, baby oil and lace scarves, he ate another chip instead of responding.

"Still, we need to get the story straight. It has to be realistic. Something that people will believe."

Ahh, there it was.

"What happened today?" he asked, wondering if he could bypass the chips and eat the guacamole with a spoon. Or his fingers.

"Today? What are you talking about?" Trying for innocent, she turned to the salad fixings she'd strewn over his counter. She set a cucumber on the cutting board and whacked it to pieces with a knife in a way that made him wince.

"Someone said something to worry you. And don't try to deny it," he said, pointing at her with the tip of his tortilla chip. "You've got that frantic, gotta-fix-it tone in your voice."

She wrinkled her nose, but didn't deny his words.

After she'd decimated the poor cucumber, she started on a carrot. Aiden shifted in his chair, wondering if there was a theme.

"Okay, so Nina and Cailley stopped by," she said, tossing the pieces into a huge bowl he didn't recognize. How much of her own stuff had she brought over? And how did she have stuff to even bring? Had she ever lived in one place long enough to collect enough to fill more than a handful of moving boxes?

"They were asking a bunch of questions. You know, when we got together, how you proposed. That kind of thing." She grimaced, setting the knife on the counter and giving him a pleading look. "I'm really bad at lying. Can't we tell them the truth? They'd keep it quiet."

Aiden was shaking his head before she even finished the plea. He'd expected the request. What he hadn't expected was his need to give her anything that would make her quit looking so worried. Nope, he told his gut. Stay strong, they had a plan and they were sticking with it.

"We established the rules. No mission can succeed if you abandon the plans at the first sign of conflict."

"These are my best friends. Not cannibal pygmies."

Aiden grinned.

"I don't know. I might classify Nina as a man-eater, and that redhead, AnaMaria? She's pretty short."

Her lips twitched, but she shook her head and plastered one of those hard-to-resist pleading looks on her face. He pretended he was immune and shook his head again.

"Look, you need to decide now, tonight, what you want." When her eyes narrowed and a naughty smile teased her mouth, he talked faster, in case she put whatever wicked thing she was thinking into words. Because knowing her, those he couldn't resist as easily.

"You need to decide what your priority is. Making your father feel better or making yourself feel better," he said, tossing the words out without thought, only aiming to make his point.

Her face seemed to crumple. Her lips trembled and her eyes widened, then filled before she blinked fast.

Shit.

"All I meant was that we need to stick with the plan," he said quickly, getting to his feet. He didn't move forward, even though his initial instinct was to offer a comforting hug.

But hugs—at least with Sage—had crossed over from innocent comfort to a danger zone. And while Aiden wasn't one to run from danger—the exact opposite in fact—he was known for strategically assessing the situation, weighing the odds and stepping in with the best weapons at his disposal.

Right now, his instincts said the situation between he and Sage was as potentially explosive as C4. So until he knew how to defuse it, and put them back on that friendly footing they'd always shared, he was keeping his hands to himself.

"You're not going to cry, are you?" he asked, knowing the suggestion would make Sage do the exact opposite.

As he'd figured, she lifted her chin and gave him a frown.

"Cry? Of course not. I was just asking if we really had to keep the truth a secret from people we trust." She shrugged, the movement sending the slinky strap of her tank top sliding over the smooth golden skin of her shoulder. Aiden's body tightened, assuring him that half a kitchen's distance between them was smart. "You trust your team, right? That's how I feel about my friends."

He almost pointed out that his team trusted each other because their lives depended on it. But the weight of the fact that sometimes, lives were lost anyway kept him from using the argument. Not because it wasn't valid. But because he knew Sage. She'd ask questions, poke and prod until she dug through the walls to the pain he'd carefully tucked away so he could deal with it. After that call from Castillo this morning, the walls were already shaky.

So he went with argument B. Logic.

"The odds of any secret being exposed are lengthened exponentially by the number of people who know the truth," he pointed out. "The Professor believes our engagement right now, because he wants to. But a few days, a week tops, and he's going to start questioning the convenience and timing."

Sage opened her mouth as if to argue, then closed it again. Brows together, she tapped the knife against the cutting board a couple of times, then gave a sideways tilt of her head to show she agreed.

"He's not going to bring his questions to you or me, Sage. He's going to observe. He's going to assess. He'll start chatting with your friends when they stop by. He won't ask them straight out, either. But he'll set verbal traps. He'll put out feelers. Your friends won't mean to, but they aren't skilled in lying. And the Professor, after decades of teaching college students, is a pro at spotting untruths. He's going to be looking, not for confirmation, but for proof that this engagement isn't real."

"That's what you'd do," she said, her words so defensive that he knew even though she wanted him to be wrong, she realized he was right. The stubborn jut of her chin echoed that, while the frustration in her eyes told him she was only arguing for form's sake.

"That's what your father will do."

After a long stare, Sage puffed out a breath, and dropped the knife onto the block

"Okay, fine," she huffed. "We won't tell anyone. Not even a hint."

"There you go," Aiden said with a satisfied nod, dropping back into his chair.

"But that means we have to get prepared."

He almost stood right back up. "What? Prepared how? For what?"

"You're right." Using her fingers, she tossed together the bowl full of chopped vegetables. "He is going to be watching. Carefully. So we have to make sure we look like a newly engaged couple."

"Are you back to that *how I proposed* garbage?" Aiden asked, tension wrapping around him so tight he could choke on it.

How the hell did a guy propose? She wasn't going to want him to pretend to have done any of that silly romantic crap, was she? On one knee, spouting soppy poetry about her eyes and moonbeams?

He gave her a narrow look and clenched his teeth. Yeah, she probably was. That was the kind of thing the dorks she usually dated would do. The kind of thing she was used to.

"Your father isn't going to be asking that kind of question," Aiden insisted, trying to shrug off the bitter taste of jealousy. Why should he care about a bunch of dorks? It wasn't as if this was a real engagement. If Sage wanted to waste herself on idiot losers, that was her problem.

"Your dad's going to want logistics," he told her. "When we saw each other last, where I was stationed and how often you came to visit. He's not going to care about the fluffy trappings."

"But my friends are. And he knows I'd share all of that with them." Using a thick dish towel, she pulled the casserole from the oven, set it on the stove top to cool then faced him again. The spicy scent of tomatoes, sausage and cheese filled the air, making Aiden's stomach growl. "He's a sociologist. He knows women share those emotional details and judge each other on them. He's also my father. He knows these are the kind of things that would matter to me, the kind I'd talk to my friends about while I was worrying over if this was the right or wrong decision."

"You do worry a lot for such a mellow person," Aiden said with a grimace. He couldn't hold the grumpy look, though. Not when whatever she'd pulled from the oven smelled so good. He couldn't remember the last home-cooked meal he'd had, but he knew he hadn't eaten anything in years that tasted as good as her dish smelled.

"Of course, my girlfriends already know the important things, even without me having to tell them."

"What important things? That I know you cheat on your healthy-eating regime with Tilly's donuts?" Who didn't know that? Hell, everyone broke down for Tilly's. Her apple fritters would even make uptight Lieutenant Banks break down and get friendly.

"No," she disagreed, bringing plates and silverware to the table. "They all agree that you're huge. So hey, we're clearly off to a good start in both the gossip category, and our wedding-night potential."

Huge? Huh? His gaze whipped from the cheese-covered dish to Sage's wicked grin.

"What?" He couldn't have heard her right.

Her dancing gaze assured him that, yes, indeed, she and her friends had talked about the size of his dick. A dick that none of them had ever seen, dammit. He had to fight back a blush.

"They were talking about our news, and compared the hugeness of it to, well, the hugeness of other things." She raised both brows, lowered her chin just a little and wriggled them toward his lap. As if he needed the help figuring out what she meant?

Well, there went his appetite.

"They didn't really ask that," he denied, more hopeful than sure. What was wrong with these women? They really talked about guys like that? How the hell did the size of his dick come into the conversation?

He peered at Sage. Did she have X-ray vision or something?

"Actually, no." She paused, just for a second. Then, as the tension started to fade in his gut, she gave him a wicked smile. "They weren't asking. They were positively stating. If we were really engaged, I might be jealous enough to want details on how my friends know so much about the state of your endowments, so to speak."

Aiden damn near put both hands over his crotch, like that'd keep its secrets.

"I've never…"

He slammed his mouth shut.

Name and rank. Don't ever offer up any more than the necessities. And in this situation, he decided the only necessity was silence.

Except for the gurgling amusement coming from the woman across from him, of course. Aiden debated glaring, but figured that'd only spur her on. Or worse, tempt her to ask for proof.

And the temptation to show her proof was growing by the second. Growing so much that he shifted his chair just a little so his legs—and other things—were under the cover of the table.

Maybe they'd be better off talking about down-on-one-knee proposals. Those didn't tempt him to strip off his clothes and offer up his body as dessert.

AIDEN WAS so damned cute.

Uptight, overthinking and way too by-the-book for her tastes. But the cuteness really did offset those things.

Sage's laughter faded but her smile stayed in place as she watched him shift in his chair. Poor guy, all that military training and living with the scratching, belching gender and you'd think he'd understand crudeness. But guys never seemed to grasp just how down and dirty women got when they were dishing on a guy. Or on his equipment.

"I thought men were big on sharing their adventures," she said with a shrug, still grinning as she mixed oil, vinegar and a few herbs in a bottle. "You know, that locker-room talk, comparing bedpost notches, that kind of thing."

"The only guys who do that are insecure assholes."

Something Aiden clearly wasn't.

Intriguing, given that they were talking both size, and talent. Her body tingled a little, both in excitement and impatience. She really, really wanted to find out about both for herself.

The size was negligible. But the talent? Her tingles took on a little extra heat. Oh, yeah. She'd bet he had a lot of talent to share. But knowing Aiden, she was going to have to ease him into that next step.

"Ahh, I see. Only assholes have to brag, then," she said with a self-deprecating smile. "That makes sense. And my dating history would prove that theory right."

Watching her pour dressing over the salad as if he were checking it for explosives, Aiden frowned and asked, "What is it with you and the losers?"

Good question. One that put quite the damper on her tingles.

"Just lucky, I guess."

"No, seriously." When he saw that she was done, he got up, crossed the room and took the salad—and the lasagna—to carry to the table. Sage stood dumbfounded, with nothing to carry herself but her glass of wine.

She'd cooked a lot of meals for guys over the years. But none had ever helped. Not even with something as simple as carrying the food to the table. Not even her father.

It wasn't that she dated sexist jerks. She was too savvy for that. More like...thoughtless, self-absorbed guys.

Which was definitely something else to think about.

Grabbing the tray of bread, oil and vinegar, she joined Aiden at the small table he'd set up in the corner of the kitchen.

"You're a gorgeous woman. Intelligent, fun, interesting. You're optimistic, open-minded and outgoing. Throw in sexy and loyal and you're almost too good to be true for most guys." Aiden scooped up a huge spoonful of lasagna, taking a bite while it was still steaming hot. His eyes closed for a second and he gave a low hum. "Throw in an excellent cook and a clever conversationalist and I just don't get it."

Wide-eyed, Sage stared. He thought she was all those things?

She'd never suffered from low self-esteem. She'd been raised to appreciate not only her gifts but to embrace what set her apart from others. It wasn't as though she didn't know she was any of those things he'd said.

But that he thought she was all that, too?

Her stomach tightened and her breath caught in her throat.

Wow.

"Just don't get what?" she asked faintly.

"I don't get why the first time you're engaged, it's to me and it's fake." He scooped up another forkful of food, this one big enough that she almost offered to get him a serving spoon to eat with. "Why do you date guys who have to stroke their sad little egos in the locker room? Who use you, instead of worship you."

She felt like her heart were made of candle wax, and it was melting all through her chest. Warm, cozy and a little stickier than she preferred to be, she bit her lip.

"Would you?"

Using the bread to sop up sauce instead of dipping it in the oil, he gave her a questioning look.

"Would I what?"

"Would you worship me?" she asked after clearing the desire out of her throat.

His hazel eyes turned molten, as if his thoughts were so hot, everything was melting. Sage's breath caught in her chest, her heart suddenly racing out of control at that look. Her thighs trembled and moisture pooled, wetting her panties.

Over just a look.

Oh, baby, that was talent. What could he do to her with a touch?

"That's not the point," he said, as always pulling that blasted control of his right back into place.

Sage wasn't sure what she wanted more.

To find out what he could do with his touch.

Or to break his control.

She knew she'd made some poor decisions in the past. She'd learned her lessons the hard way and paid plenty of consequences for those decisions.

Nothing in life was free. Especially things that were

extra tempting. But after a while, a girl got good at weighing the costs against the pleasure her decision might offer.

The cost of going after Aiden could be more than she could afford.

She didn't care.

She wanted him. Wanted him more than she'd ever wanted anything. Anyone.

Maybe it was the distraction factor. The only time she wasn't miserable with worry over her father was when she was with Aiden. She didn't know if that was because he made her feel safe, like nothing bad could happen if he was around. Or if it was the constant state of sexual energy zinging through her body, short-circuiting her worry zones.

Or maybe it was the whole fake engagement thing. Playing the part, everybody thinking they were really engaged. That they were really free to have all the sex together they wanted, sanctioned by the promise of a ring and a piece of paper.

Or maybe it was because this was the most she'd spent time with Aiden since they were teenagers. And really the first time she'd seen him as more than her dad's sidekick or her geeky sort-of friend. Now he was a sexy guy. A navy SEAL who had an air of danger about him that said he could kick any butt out there. And the rock-hard muscles to back that claim up nicely.

She wet her lips, noting the play of those muscles as he plowed his way through the lasagna.

"Aren't you having any?" he asked.

"Oh, I'd love to. It looks delicious," she said without thinking. Brows drawing together, she raised her gaze to his. "Having any what?"

"Dinner? Food?" He gestured with his fork to the already half-empty tray. "Lasagna?"

Oh. That.

Confused, and not liking it, Sage absently spooned a scoop onto her plate, then ate a bite.

"Is it as delicious as you thought?" he asked.

"I think I need to taste more before I decide."

Before he could put into words the frown that slid across his face, she set her fork down, clasped her hands together and leaned forward.

"So, let's talk about being engaged."

"Are you back to that?" He sounded weary, his body language screaming *let it go already*. But Sage knew better. This was important. For more reasons than she was willing to admit.

"Don't you think it's important?" she asked instead. Seeing the stubborn look on his face, she changed tactics, shifting to words she knew he'd resonate with. "If you're going on a mission, you'd know as much about your target as possible, wouldn't you? You'd learn the terrain, know the language, observe the locals so you could blend."

For just a second, his gaze heated and his eyes traveled over her body, as if assessing her terrain. She almost told him she liked her language a little naughty and suggested which body parts they should blend, but managed to clamp that behind her lips at the last moment.

His eyes met hers again, the expression in them guarded. Then he shrugged.

"Fine. We'll talk about it after dinner."

All the better. Attempting to seduce him on a table filled with food wasn't her idea of sexy.

Sexy would be finding out how he liked it. If he was always in command, and how hard it'd be to break his control. Did he have to be on top? Or was he into experimenting?

More than ready to start finding out, Sage pushed her

plate away. She gestured to the casserole dish, but he shook his head, indicating he didn't want a fourth helping.

"You didn't eat much," he observed, leaning back in his chair and giving her a worried look. "Are you okay?"

"Sure. Maybe. I don't know." She shrugged, getting to her feet to gather dishes. She needed to move. To do something productive. Before she did something crazy. "I'm distracted, I guess."

"Worrying about your dad?"

"Yeah. About my dad, and about this whole engagement thing," she said, setting the dishes in the sink. Before she could rinse, he was there with the salad bowl and mostly empty casserole dish.

She eyed his still-flat belly. Where did he put all that food?

"You cooked," he told her. "I'll do the dishes."

"You'll…"

"Yeah, don't worry about them now," he said, wrapping his fingers around her upper arm to gently move her away from the sink. "Let's get this engagement issue nailed down so you can relax."

Relax?

Well, if they nailed it—or he nailed her—the way she wanted, she'd definitely be relaxing.

6

SAGE MULLED OVER the different ways she'd like to work up to relaxation while brewing coffee. She'd insisted, since she wanted a few minutes to think before they had their little conversation. Stepping through the kitchen, her hands filled with her favorite brew, she took a deep breath.

The living room, like the kitchen and the rest of the small house, was just this side of bare, with only enough stuff in it to claim that it wasn't vacant.

Even bare, though, the house had charm. Rough-hewn high-beam ceilings, plaster walls and arched doorways gave it a cottage feel. The tiny kitchen with its antique stove and butcher-block island, the cozy living room with the windows flanking the wide fireplace.

Facing that wall was a long, hand-me-down couch she remembered from his parents' house. Remembered jumping on like it was a trampoline, to be exact. She gave it an assessing look. Those cushions might still have some good bounce in them.

Excitement swirled in her tummy and her breath hitched a little.

Time to find out.

"Coffee?" she asked, lifting the tray. "I brought my favorite roast, and a few different flavored oils in case you wanted to try something exotic."

Oh, please, let him be down for trying exotic. Or kinky. Or, heck, she'd settle for just a little naughty.

"Black is fine. I don't like any of that strange stuff with my coffee."

Booooring. Sage wrinkled her nose, but poured him a plain ole, nothing-exotic coffee. She handed him the drink. Their fingers brushed, giving her enough of a tingle to make up for the lack of excitement in the cup.

She added a hint of hazelnut and a dollop of whipped chocolate to hers, then joined him on the couch. The cushion gave just a little bounce when she sat, making her smile.

This could definitely get interesting.

"Some of my friends already asked about the ring," she said before sipping her coffee.

"What'd you tell them?"

"That you were still searching for the perfect one." She held out her left hand and wiggled her fingers. "I said you'd probably find one in some exotic locale while on duty, and that would make it extra special."

He gave a laughing sort of shake of his head, then nodded to let her know he'd go along with the story.

"Okay, so how did we get engaged?" he asked, his tone making it clear that he was humoring her.

"Well, it needs to be realistic," she decided, sipping her drink. She paused to lick the whipped chocolate off her upper lip, liking the way his gaze followed her move.

She was tempted to do it again. But if she moved too fast, Aiden would figure out her seduction plans. With some guys, that was okay. They'd either take it as a compliment, let it stroke their ego, or immediately reciprocate.

Aiden, she figured, would get up and walk away.

Not the kind of seduction reaction a girl usually aimed for.

Better to take a page out of his book. To go for some stealth seduction. A little recon, a little strategy, then move in for the hit.

"What if you were on leave on a beach somewhere, maybe Borneo or Fiji. You're walking along the water at sunset, and you see a woman resting on the sand. Face-down, nude, sleeping so peacefully that you slow so as not to disturb her." Sage shifted, arching her back as if she were feeling the setting sun on her bare skin. "Then, you feel this energy. This recognition deep in your heart."

She ignored his eye roll, curling one leg under her as she got into a comfier position to weave her fantasy.

"Before you can decide whether to say something or move on, she lifts her head. Her hair slides over her face, but you recognize her. Your eyes meet. Sparks fly. Instantly, you both realize that this moment, this place, is everything you've been waiting for."

"Right." He rolled his eyes again. "That moment?"

"And that place," she confirmed, smiling over his amused sarcasm. "So happy to see each other, you run together, hugging tight."

"But she, I mean, you are still naked, right?"

Oh. Sage wrinkled her nose. Good point.

No problem. She could still make it work.

"The emotions quickly change, moving from excitement to seeing each other to excitement to do each other." She waved her hand between their bodies, as if he needed clarification of which other he was doing. "Passion overtakes common sense. You fall together to the sand, rolling, kissing, exploring each other's bodies."

"In the sand?"

This time she was the one who rolled her eyes.

"Okay, fine. You fall together onto her beach blanket,

rolling and kissing and exploring. You get so carried away, you make love there on the beach, as the sun sets over the ocean."

"We're paying attention to the sunset during all of this?"

"Well, you are a SEAL. You have some kind of internal sensors that tell you when these things happen," she tossed back.

He snorted, shaking his head before gesturing that she should go on.

"Afterward, even though your knees are weak with the power of our lovemaking..." She paused to thump him on the back when he choked on a swallow of coffee. "You wrap me in the blanket, carry me back to your room and we spend the rest of the week in a frenzy of sexual delights."

"Your father is going to love this story," he said in a contemplative tone. "Too bad we didn't have pictures to share."

"The camera fell in the hot tub or we would have an album full."

"Nice."

"Okay, fine," she said waving her hand to shoo away his objections. "So this is the naughty, detailed version our friends hear. They aren't going to share the sex stuff with my dad. But their smirks will go a long way toward convincing him, don't you think?"

"That we had sex, maybe."

She shivered at the way he said that, the words husky and low. Good. He might not be loving it, but at least he wasn't unaffected by her little scenario if his voice was any indication. And his voice was all she had to go on, given that he was an expert and keeping the stoic face. And he was sitting sideways in loose slacks, damn him.

"Okay, but the sex was so good, so mind-blowing, so amazingly out of this world—"

"We've covered the sex part," he interrupted.

Sage's lips twitched.

"Okay, on to the engagement part. So, you were completely heartbroken over the idea of tearing yourself away from me, even after a week of constantly being inside of me, that you couldn't leave. Oh, you told me you were. I was brave, holding back my tears until you were gone," she said, lifting her chin and looking as brave as she could. He rolled his eyes, making her laugh.

"Because you know tears would make it harder for me to leave?"

"No, because I get all splotchy when I cry. There's no way I'd want the last view you had of me before you went back on duty to be my face all swollen and mottled with a red rash."

"Gotcha."

Sage took a sip of her coffee, then pressed her palm to her chest in her most dramatic fashion. And smiled when his eyes followed the movement, his gaze darkening at the sight of her nipples beading beneath the silk of her tank top. The nubs tightened even more as she took a deep breath, the fabric gently sliding over them as she imagined his fingers would.

"So, splotchiness aside, what next?" he prodded after clearing his throat.

"Next?" Next she wanted to rip her clothes off, lie across the coffee table and invite him in for some covert operations.

"Yeah. You are crying, thinking I'm gone. Then what?"

"Um, then what…" She took a deep breath, trying to pull her focus off the coffee table and back to the fantasy. "Um, okay, so then I'm having dinner, alone at a small table on a restaurant balcony and you show up."

"You weren't so brokenhearted that you lost your appetite?"

"I never lose my appetite." For anything. "So you show up, you sweep me into your arms and, over my delighted giggles, you carry me across the beach, up the side of a mountain where you set me down and point to the sand."

Aiden opened his mouth as if to protest, then shook his head and gestured that she keep talking.

"Spelled out in rocks across the beach are the words, *Sage, will you marry me,*" she finished in her most dramatic tone. Which probably lost a little of its edge when she giggled at the end.

Aiden stared for so long, she wondered if he was running some kind of top secret mental background check of her personal history to see if she'd ever actually been proposed to like that. Since Sage had spent most of her dating life making sure the guys she went out with were more commitment-phobic than she was, she knew the answer he'd find was a big fat no.

"As interesting as that would be," he finally said, his voice gruff enough to assure her that he was very, very interested. "I don't think anyone is going to believe I'd go AWOL to carry you to the top of a mountain."

"No?"

"Let's try something just a little more traditional."

Pulling a face, Sage set her coffee on the burl table and shrugged.

"Okay, fine. You took me to dinner at a nice restaurant, toasted me with pricey champagne, and hid the ring—which I still don't have, by the way—in a slice of cake that was served for dessert."

"I said traditional, not cliché."

Oooh, interesting distinction.

She leaned one arm along the back of the couch, the

nubby fabric rough against the soft flesh of her underarm. Her fingers were centimeters away from his shoulder, but she didn't touch. Not yet.

"Why don't you tell me what you consider traditional then," she invited quietly.

The setting sun cast a warm, orange glow over the room, highlighting his features as he looked at her. His eyes were intense, but a smile played around the corners of his mouth.

"I consider a traditional proposal to be romantic. Not something that can be copied from a movie," he said, his shrug just a little uncomfortable. As if admitting that he'd ever seen a romantic proposal in a movie put his man-card in danger. "Romantic is something that suits the couple. You know, it's personal."

"What kind of proposal would suit us?" Unable to resist any longer, her fingers trailed along his shoulder, soft as a whisper. "If we were a couple, of course."

"A coded letter sent from an aircraft carrier to a commune on a mountain in Tibet?" he suggested.

"Try again," Sage suggested with narrowed eyes, not sure if he was actually teasing. "I think you might have missed the romance angle with that scenario."

"What if it was a secret code using romantic movie titles?" he asked, frowning.

Sage gave an amused groan. She knew that look wasn't because she'd dissed the romance of his scenario. Nope. This was what Aiden did. He got an idea, then he obsessed with it until he found a way to make it work.

Which meant that somehow, some way, this code was going to be a part of their engagement story. Her dad would like that. So they might as well make it a fun one.

But, later.

She shifted, making a show of setting her cup on the

table and surreptitiously inching just a little closer so their knees brushed.

Right now, she had other things she wanted to clarify.

Like how good her hotshot SEAL was with his hands. His mouth. And any other parts of his body that she might get her hands on.

AIDEN WAS PRETTY SURE that Sage wasn't deliberately trying to kill him. She might be flighty and a little self-absorbed from time to time, but she didn't have a mean bone in her body.

She did, however, have a whole lot of gorgeous, sexy bones, covered with enticing silky flesh. Temptingly soft hair that slid like a golden waterfall over her shoulder, trailing down to curl at the tip of her breast. A breast he wanted to touch. To weigh in the curve of his hand before tasting.

And now, on top of all of that, she was talking sex with him? Painting a fantasy about the two of them, a week-long love-fest on the beach? Hot-tubbing?

She might not be trying to kill him, but his body just might if he didn't do something—soon—to relieve a little of the pressure she'd stirred up.

Which meant she needed to leave.

"Dinner was great, and the coffee the best I've ever had," he said, draining his before toasting her with the empty cup. "But we should call it a night. I'm still dragging a little, and could use some sleep."

Damn.

Aiden knew the words were a mistake before they'd finished crossing his lips. He didn't need her eyes lighting up or to see the delighted smile spread across her face to know he'd just opened the wrong door.

"I'll bet you are," she said, patting his knee gently, her fingers lingering long enough to make sure he appreciated the loss of them when she pulled away. "You travel so much, do you even get jet lag anymore? Or are you simply accustomed to setting your own time zone?"

Grinning, he gave a rueful shake of his head. He should have known better than to expect Sage to do the expected.

"I traveled from Coronado to Villa Rosa," he reminded her. Of course, he'd traveled from Africa to San Diego two days before that, but that was need-to-know information. "The only difference in time zones is going from military time to Pacific time."

"Ahh, so no jet-lag issues, just general tiredness. I can see how you'd be needing to rest up, given how hard you're always pushing and working."

Aiden shrugged, as if it wasn't a big deal. That was his job, after all. But something inside him warmed, softened. Had anyone ever understood that before? His need to decompress, to take a few days to step out of his role as a machine and learn to be a man again?

Just Sage.

"Then again, the sun hasn't even set yet," she said, tilting her head toward the still-light yard visible from the window.

Ahh, there it was.

"Sage—"

"So why don't we wind this evening up, quickly, so you can rest," she said, talking right over his protest with a big, bright smile. "That way, none of it will be weighing on your mind, keeping you awake."

Right. Because he wasn't going to be up all night—in every sense of the word—reliving that little fantasy she'd woven earlier? Still, she had a point.

Aiden sighed, inclining his head for her to continue.

"You know after tonight, we're not going to get a ton of

privacy. My dad wants his illness kept quiet, so we're going to be the focus of attention. Invitations, questions, teasing."

"Goody," he deadpanned.

Her eyes lit up.

"Goody, indeed. But that does bring us back to the reason for our visit tonight. We need to make sure we not only have our stories straight, but we also have to walk the talk. You know what I mean?"

Yeah. She meant they weren't done yet.

At least, she didn't think they were. Aiden had other ideas, though.

"We'll be fine," he told her.

"Don't you think it's a good idea to practice a little?" she asked, her fingers tracing along his shoulder, leaving tiny trails of fire that burned right through the fabric of his shirt. "You know, so we don't look awkward when we do it in front of people."

"I know it's a big turn-on for some people, but I'm really not a fan of having sex in front of other people."

Was Sage?

Aiden had never thought of himself as the jealous type. He had never cared enough about a woman to commit his emotions, or to want any sort of exclusivity. In or out of bed, physically or voyeuristically.

But Sage was different.

As much as he'd love to watch her being pleasured—by him. Or pleasuring herself—for him. But sex, with others watching?

His muscles tensed, adrenaline rushing his system right into fight mode.

Nope.

Others weren't invited.

Feeling like his control fuse blew, Aiden knew he was

about to make a major mistake. But without that fuse, he couldn't help it. The need was too much.

His eyes locked on hers as he shifted forward. His hand cupped the soft curve of her neck. Her misty blue-green gaze was both soothing and exciting as Sage's eyes widened, then softened in anticipation.

He took her mouth.

Without warning, without fanfare, he simply leaned in and kissed her. Soft and welcoming, her lips parted easily at the sweep of his tongue.

She tasted so good. Like coffee and something exotic.

She felt even better. Soft lips, hot mouth, her tongue entwined with his with ease, as if they'd been kissing this way all their lives.

The excitement was new, though.

It pounded through Aiden with a power he'd never felt before. It ripped at his control, shredded his intentions.

It simply took over.

She slid closer. Or he pulled her over. He had no idea which. He just knew that she was there, almost in his lap. Close enough for him to skim his hands over her side, to revel in the smooth silk of her skin as his knuckles brushed along the inside of her arm.

He reached her waist, curving his palm over her hip for one second, then slid his hand back up. He stopped just short of her breast, his hand along her side and his thumb curving under the full temptation.

But not touching.

"Mmm," she murmured against his mouth. "You're good at that."

"We're good," he returned without thinking.

"What other kind of kissing are you good at?" she asked, her words so low and husky they were more a vibration against his lips than an actual sound.

"What kind do you like?" he asked, his tongue tracing her bottom lip.

Since even a breath was too long to wait to taste more of her, Aiden slid his lips along her jaw, placing tiny kisses on her chin, then following the curve of her throat. She arched her neck, shifting her head to the side.

A smart man, he didn't hesitate in accepting her invitation.

He ran his tongue along her collarbone, before burying his face in the curve of her shoulder. She tasted so damned good.

He breathed deep, one hand burrowing into her hair to keep her from moving. She smelled even better. Like green grass and wildflowers.

Her fingers teased, tiny swirls down the back of his head, over his neck and across his shoulders. She scraped her nails, light and tempting, over his biceps. Aiden wanted to flex just to impress her. Hell, half of his body was already flexing in appreciation. Since she was rubbing her foot along his calf, the movement snuggling her thigh against his happily flexing dick, he figured she was appreciating already.

But was she impressed?

He'd never been the kind of guy to show off. Secure in who he was, what he was, Aiden always figured people could take him or leave him, he didn't care either way.

But right now, for the first time, he was desperate to make an impression.

He, and his dick.

He wanted Sage to be awed, blown away. He wanted her to feel the same raging, desperate passion that was pounding through him.

With that in mind, he let loose the rigid control he'd

held over his body, over his desire. Over his mind. And just let go.

His hand shifted. It only needed to move an inch, and he had her breast beneath his fingers.

God, she felt good.

Full, soft, her nipple beaded and hardened against his palm.

Their kiss exploded.

Hot, wild, it went over the edge, taking Aiden with it.

Tongues battled, his hands raced over her body. She was so soft, but so firm. Long limbs gave way to gentle curves.

One hand still cupping her breast, his palm rubbing her nipple, the other slipped under her skirt. Up the hot, silky length of her thigh. Her legs shifted, just enough to offer an invitation higher.

An invitation he couldn't resist.

Not letting himself think, Aiden grabbed her by the waist and moved, lightning fast, to lay her out on the coffee table. His mouth still on hers, he skimmed his fingers under that skirt, pushing the silky mass up to her waist and with one quick tug, ripped her panties out of the way.

She gasped against his lips, then gave a delighted laugh.

"More," she demanded.

More indeed.

He wasn't a stupid man. He knew this was going to complicate the hell out of everything. But he felt so good. So connected. He was pretty sure this was the best he'd ever felt, and he knew if he kept going it was only going to get better.

Aiden wanted better.

Skipping the niceties, desperate to taste her, Aiden slid down her body. He paused for a long moment to revel in the sight of her, spread out for his pleasure. Wet, pink and delicate, she was gorgeous.

He leaned in, tracing her damp bud with his finger. She jerked, then shifted her legs to wrap her knees over his shoulders and pull him closer.

He loved how she made her wants crystal clear.

The least he could do was meet them.

With that in mind, Aiden bent low between her thighs. Using his tongue and fingers, he worshipped her in ways he'd fantasized about so many times. Her reaction was even better than his imagination, though. She went up so fast, responded so intently, he felt like a sex god.

Then she exploded.

Her back arched off the table, the muscles of her thighs tight against his shoulders as she went over. Her panting cries of delight, combined with her fingers digging into his shoulders almost sent him over the edge with her.

Damn, he realized with a rare feeling of fear. He could see where this kind of thing would lead to him carrying her up some damned mountain to stare at some stupid rocks, spelling out a crazy marriage proposal.

Sage shimmied out from under him, off the table.

"Hey, I wasn't finished," he objected.

She laughed, pointing at the couch in silent demand. After a low growl, Aiden sat down, waiting to see what she'd do next. He hoped she'd do it without her underwear. There was something extra sexy about knowing she was bare under that flowing silk.

Bare and wet.

She dropped to her knees between his legs, gazing up at him as she tossed her hair back over her shoulder. With her eyes locked on his, she first traced her index finger along his rock-hard erection. Then, pulling her lower lip between her teeth, she unsnapped and unzipped his pants.

He swore his dick gave a groan of relief at the sudden freedom as it sprang up, pushing his boxers to their limit.

"Oh, my," she breathed as she watched the move, her words a reverent whisper. "Looks like those rumors were right."

Aiden would have laughed, but he was too busy drowning in lust. The sight of her, bent so low over his lap that her hair trailed across his thighs, was straight out of one of his hottest fantasies.

Her fingers trailed along his erection, a worshipful touch that was so light, so delicious, he almost exploded right then. Her eyes met his, wicked delight dancing in the depths of her aquamarine gaze.

She was incredible.

She was addicting.

She was trouble.

And Aiden wasn't sure he could handle her kind of trouble.

At war with himself, he watched her head descend. His body craved her like an addict craved a fix. It was that desperate need that pulled his brain out of the sexual fog.

Before her lips could make contact, though, he shifted aside.

The minute she touched him, they'd have to finish this. It'd go from pleasure to commitment.

And he couldn't—wouldn't—go further until he knew what he was committing to.

"We need to stop," he growled, tucking himself back behind the safety of his zipper.

His body wanted to know what the hell he was doing.

His mind was trying to figure out what the hell he'd been thinking.

He couldn't answer either one.

All he could do was distance himself from the needs pounding through him. Using the same technique he employed when he was wounded in battle to disassociate himself from his body, Aiden started reciting Virgil in Latin.

"Aiden?"

"Hang on." Another three verses and he had control. Two more and he was able to take a deep, cleansing breath and open his eyes. He turned his head, looking at Sage.

She hadn't moved.

Still sitting on the edge of the table, her braless breasts pressing against the wet silk and her skirt bunched at the top of her thighs, she was the image of temptation.

He closed his eyes and started reciting again.

"Aiden?"

"This is a bad idea. We need to *not* be doing this," he said, his eyes still closed as he gestured between them.

"But it feels so good," she purred.

He didn't have to open his eyes to know she was stretching across the table like a sensuous cat, just waiting to be petted again.

God, he wanted to pet her.

"It could ruin our relationship. And as a by-product, my relationship with the Professor," he said, using the argument that was now looping through his brain. The only one that had any impact.

Clearly it had an impact on Sage, too.

He heard the rustle of fabric, the shifting of her body as she got off the table. After a few seconds, long enough for her to find her panties and put them back on, he felt it safe to open his eyes.

Damn, she was sexy.

Her skin still flushed with passion and her hair in disarray over her shoulders, she looked like exactly what she was. A delicious woman who'd been worshipped by a very appreciative man's lips.

His lips tingled to get back to the worshipping.

"You're sure about this?" she asked quietly, her fingers on the hem of her blouse as if she was ready to pull it off at the slightest indication from him.

"I'm sure," Aiden said. And he was.

Painfully, miserably, regrettably sure.

Sex between them would be crossing a line they could never return from.

It'd change everything.

He was trying to figure out what mattered. Where he belonged. Until he was clear on that, he couldn't risk ruining everything for sex.

Not even incredible, mind-blowing, body-melting sex with the most intriguingly sensuous, amazingly addicting woman he knew.

He waited for Sage to get pissed.

Or worse, act hurt.

Please, don't let her cry. He cringed inside, knowing her tears were going to slay him.

But being Sage, she didn't do the expected. Instead of anger or sadness, she offered him a bright smile, brushed a kiss over his chin and patted his cheek.

Like he was some freaking little kid or something.

Aiden scowled.

"Your call," she said, heading for the door. "But if we're not going to do the deed, I should get home. We'll talk tomorrow, okay?"

That's it? She wasn't upset?

It didn't mean *anything* to her?

"You're really okay with this?" Why did that bother him so much? Was that his ego whining? Or something deeper?

"Okay with you being allowed to decide if you want to have sex or not?" Eyes wide, she made a tut-tutting noise and shook her head. "Seriously? Isn't that a double standard?"

"I made you come with my fingers and tongue," he pointed out, shoving his hands in his pockets to keep from grabbing her to do it again. Maybe she needed a reminder.

"And it was quite delicious, thank you," she assured him, laughing. "Aiden, do you want me to be upset that you don't think sex between us is a good idea? Should I pout or throw things?"

It sounded stupid when she said it like that.

But, well, yeah.

"Sweetie." She crossed the room, close enough to touch. But she kept her hands to herself, so just her scent wrapped around him. "You know me better than that. I'm not going to emotionally manipulate you. We're both operating under complete free will here. Isn't that what you go out and defend? Our right to freedom."

"So you're totally cool with the fact that this—" he waved his hand back and forth between them "—that anything physical between us is over. That we'll never be having sex with each other."

She sucked in a quick breath, her beautiful eyes rounding before she bit her lip. She looked away, blinking fast, then took a couple more deep breaths.

Aww, shit. Now he'd done it. She was going to cry.

Her eyes damp, Sage pressed her lips tight together. But, apparently unable to hold back, she burst into laughter.

The woman was seriously killing him.

"What's so damned funny?"

"You actually think you're going to be able to resist this heat between us for long?" She shook her head in a pitying sort of way. "There's no way that's going to happen. Sooner or later, you'll sort through all those thoughts running through your head. You'll justify your body's demands. And then you'll find me."

What he'd do when he found her went unspoken.

But they both glanced at the table, then looked at each other again.

What he'd do was perfectly clear.

He wanted to deny her words. To tell her that she was completely wrong.

But just like she didn't emotionally manipulate, he didn't lie.

So he chose valor by discretion and clamped his lips shut.

From the way her eyes danced, she probably read his thoughts and was calculating how long it'd take before he gave in.

"It's going to be fine," she promised quietly, stepping away. Aiden didn't breathe easy until she'd put eight feet between them, though. Far enough that her scent was just a promise and that he couldn't quickly grab her back.

"In the meantime, now I can assure all my friends the rumors were right. That you are, in fact, huge," she said wickedly before sashaying toward the door. Once there, she turned, gave a little finger wave, and was gone.

Aiden waited until he saw her clear the front porch before he laughed.

Then he headed for an icy-cold shower.

<u>7</u>

AIDEN HAD ONCE SPENT a week traveling through a swamp with a piece of shrapnel lodged in his shoulder.

That'd been a piece of cake compared to this last week, playing the other half of Happily Engaged Couple opposite Sage. Like now, at the fancy engagement dinner the Professor had put together. He'd thrown open the doors to the house on the hill, catered a delicious meal and invited everyone he, Aiden or Sage knew to celebrate his delight.

But as hard as it was to celebrate something fake, the joy and peace on the old man's face made it totally worthwhile.

So, nope. It wasn't the pretending that was difficult.

Nor, surprisingly, was it spending a lot of time with Sage. She was pretty awesome. Fun, funny, easy to talk to, easier to listen to. Her view of the world was both bright and optimistic, but so down-to-earth real that it made Aiden pause and reconsider some of his own views.

Nope. What was hard was the memory of their little coffee-table encounter that was killing him. The vivid recollection of Sage's body beneath his. The taste of her was still there on his tongue, the sound of her moans whispered in his ear.

It was the most incredible sex he'd ever *almost* had. And he refused to do it again.

Yep. That was the hard part.

That, and his dick. He'd been in a constant state of arousal since Sage had greeted him in that tiny bikini of hers.

He peered across the room at Sage. Despite the crowd, she was easy to spot. As tall as most of the men, taller in those spiked heels, she glowed. Her dress was some kind of flowing aqua fabric that swept over her body like a waterfall from the tiny straps at her shoulders all the way to the ragged hem at her knees.

His fingers itched to touch that fabric, to see if it was as silky as her skin. His mouth watered for a taste like he was a starving man and she a feast.

He wondered if she'd wear that bikini again anytime soon.

Hey, if a guy was gonna be chronically horny, he might as well enjoy the inspiration.

"Great party, dude."

"I hate these things," Aiden muttered into his beer. He hated wearing suits even more. So much so that he only owned one. A wool much too heavy for April in California that he'd found in the back of his closet.

"At least your future father-in-law kept it mellow. My engagement party we wore monkey suits." Gary tugged at the cuffs of his own suit and grunted. Then he gave Aiden a questioning look. "Except you, who if I recall wore your dress whites."

"My uniforms are back on base. Sage and I were planning to keep our engagement a secret, so I didn't think I'd have need of them," Aiden said, using the story he and Sage had settled on. That they'd figured, given both of their lifestyles, to give their engagement a while to settle before telling people. So far, nobody who knew them had questioned that.

Aiden shifted his shoulders, wishing the fabric would stretch a little. Neither the suit nor the situation were a good fit. But he hadn't been willing to wear his navy dress uniform to a fake engagement party. Lying was bad enough. Doing so in uniform would feel sacrilegious.

"You're a lucky guy," Gary said, not for the first time. He gestured, not to Sage, though, but to her father. "You're on great terms with your future in-law. Having a hot wife is all well and good, but it's the in-laws that can make your life heaven or hell."

Aiden ripped his gaze away from Sage's laughing face, searching the crowd to find the Professor. He was cozied up with Dr. Brooke, the two men looking pleased with themselves. The almost-empty glasses of brandy in their hands might play into that. But more likely, it was that the Professor was reacting really well to the experimental treatment. And, of course, to his daughter's engagement.

"He's a great guy," Aiden said, gesturing with his beer toward the older man.

"He feels the same. It's always a toss-up who he's going to be bragging on more when he corners someone on the street. You, or his daughter."

"His daughter," Aiden said automatically. "Why wouldn't it be?"

Gary gave him an *are you kidding* look.

"Um, no offense to your fiancée, but it's not like she's racking up the bragging points."

"She spent last summer volunteering for the Peace Corps," Aiden pointed out. "She's on a dozen charitable boards, all focused on helping the needy. She spends time at three hospitals doing that Reiki stuff of hers. She grew a community garden in Seattle, taught art at a women's shelter in New Orleans and fostered kittens in Phoenix."

"Dude, you got it bad."

What?

Aiden replayed his own words.

Crap.

He sounded like a lovesick idiot.

He could try to tell himself that he was just getting into the role, but he'd forgotten he was playing a part in that little defensive rant.

But he hated lying. To himself.

That didn't mean he had to have a serious heart-to-heart with himself either. He could simply accept that he admired Sage.

He glanced across the room again. And sighed. There were so, so many things to admire about her. As if she had a special radar that let her know when he had hit his limit—in partying and in horniness—Sage glanced over. She said something to the group she was with, touching Nina's hand briefly. Then she made her way over to the corner where Aiden and Gary were leaning.

"Hiding, gentlemen?" she teased when she reached them.

"Enjoying the view of my wife from afar is all," Gary shot back. "And now I'll go ask her to dance and leave you two lovebirds alone."

"Mmm, lovebirds?" Sage said, sidling close to Aiden's side and sliding him a laughing look. "We're doing good."

He grunted.

"Dad looks so happy, doesn't he? He even danced with me. He hasn't done that since I was twelve and he was teaching me the swing."

He grunted.

"All in all, it's gone pretty well. And I think after this

things will mellow out. Especially as we've told everyone we're looking at a long engagement. They've even stopped asking me about wedding plans and shopping for a dress."

Aiden grunted again.

"You are such a chatterbox tonight," Sage said, wrapping her hand around his bicep and cuddling close as she gave him a big, wide-eyed smile. "Slow down, let me get a word in edgewise."

He almost grunted again, but her arch look warned him that she might do something drastic if he did. Violence, he could handle. But Sage was more a lover than a fighter. And that might be more dangerous than he wanted to deal with.

"Your dad seems like he had a good night," he said instead. "Actually it's been a good week, hasn't it? He's looking a lot more energetic and healthy than when we got home."

"Dr. Brooke said he's responding much better than they'd expected," Sage said quietly, leaning her head against his shoulder as she followed his gaze. "Still, he's talking about retiring. The only thing keeping him from telling the university is that he's holding out for the perfect replacement."

"You gotta admire the guy." Aiden shook his head. "He's fighting for his health and he's worried about hand-picking his successor."

"That's not necessarily a bad thing," she said with a laugh. "He told Mrs. Green that he'd always dreamed that you'd eventually take the job. Given that you don't even have your PhD, and that you've got a pretty intense career going already, he'll be hanging around a lot of years waiting for that dream to come true."

"I wouldn't need my PhD to take over," Aiden said automatically. "At least, not at first. Dean Schumer mentioned it a few days ago."

Sage looked up, confusion and something else in her eyes. He couldn't tell if it was worry or excitement, she blinked it away so fast.

"You talked to the dean about teaching at the university?"

"No. The dean talked to me about someday, after I leave the service, considering it." A consideration that, for some crazy reason, was holding more appeal than Aiden would have expected.

"You'd move back here after you were done in the navy?" Sage asked, her frown making Aiden nervous for some reason. Not because she looked like she was up to something. But because he had this sudden need, deep in his gut, to convince her that it was a good idea.

Something he wasn't actually sure of himself.

"Looks like we might be ready to call it a night," he noted, glad to change the subject as he nodded toward her father. Then he frowned. Ten minutes ago, the Professor had been smiling and looking hearty. Now he looked worn and gray.

Aiden glanced at Sage. Crap. She looked devastated. His mind raced, searching for something comforting to distract her. He came up blank.

Shit.

When she took a shaky breath, he did the only thing he could.

He leaned down and kissed her.

After a second of surprise, she enthusiastically leaned into him and gave a low hum of appreciation.

Damn, she tasted good.

So good it took a couple of wolf whistles before Aiden could pull himself away.

"Mmm," Sage murmured, blinking slowly up at him as if reluctantly coming out of a trance. "That was nice."

"Look at the two of you," the Professor said with a hearty laugh, patting Aiden on the shoulder. "You're going to be so happy together."

A cheer worked its way through the room, then died away as the older man offered a quiet toast. Then the Professor gave everyone his best wishes. He kissed his daughter, then gave Aiden's hand a firm shake and serene smile before he excused himself to leave for bed and let the younger crowd enjoy themselves.

His departure seemed to be a signal of some kind. Half the guests departed within five minutes, leaving Aiden and Sage's circle of friends.

Each and every one of them wearing a gleeful look of trouble on their faces.

"What's going on?" Aiden murmured to Sage as they returned from walking the last guest to the door.

"Dunno."

"Surprise," called out the dozen people left in the room.

"You were all here already," Sage said with a laugh. "Aren't you supposed to, oh, I don't know, surprise us before you say that?"

"It's a preemptive surprise," Nina said, pulling a tote bag from behind her back. "This is the traditional engagement treat. The two of you missed all the fun the last few years, but you'll catch on fast."

"What in the hell are you talking about?" Aiden eyed the slinky fabric the brunette was hauling out of her bag and shook his head. "We didn't ask for a treat."

"You don't have to ask. It's our gift to you," Gary said, grinning. "We tie you up, blindfold you, haul you off someplace romantic, then pick you up again tomorrow night."

One, two, four, six guys, eight women and some determined smiles. Shoving his hands in his pockets, Aiden sighed. This wasn't going to be pretty.

"All of you?" Sage asked faintly, her eyes moving from person to person, before she gave Aiden a baffled look. "What if this isn't a good time?"

"You're all packed, your dad knows you'll be gone," Cailley told her as she took a couple of the scarves and made a twirling motion with her finger to indicate that they turn around. "Now come along quietly or we'll get ugly."

"Aiden is a SEAL," Sage said, looking baffled and confused, as if the idea of a roomful of guys thinking they could take him was beyond her comprehension. "You don't think you can make him do anything he doesn't want to, do you?"

Aiden had shaken hands with the president of the United States and been thanked for a job well done once. He'd received a number of commendations and medals. He was pretty sure none of that stacked up against the feeling of pride glowing in his chest at that moment, knowing Sage thought he could take on this entire room.

She was right, he acknowledged, eyeing the group. The only one who was any real challenge was Gary, and the guy couldn't even jog outdoors.

Still, hurting friends was never a good idea.

"Nah, we're not crazy enough to think we can take Aiden," Nina said with a wave of her hand. "But we are loud, and would yell a lot if you didn't go along peacefully."

The truth about the Professor's health wasn't being broadcast, but Aiden figured most people here had guessed there was something wrong. Enough people to make that threat a viable one.

"That's blackmail," Sage observed, obviously reaching the same conclusion.

"Yep," Aiden agreed with a sigh. It only took him a brief moment to calculate the options. "Might as well go along."

It'd be easier to get out of whatever the group had planned once they were at a different location. Again, on the same wavelength as him, after a brief glance at him Sage heaved a huge, dramatic sigh, held out both wrists to the crowd and tossed back her head.

"Fine. Take us away," she instructed.

And away they were taken. Blindfolded, escorted to a minivan, of all things, and if Aiden's instincts were right—and they always were—driven five miles to the east before being escorted into, from what he could tell from looking out the bottom of his blindfold, a small resort hotel.

Apparently having already checked in, someone opened the hotel room door.

"Go ahead and take off your scarves," Gary ordered, giving them a gentle push inside.

At his limit of playing nice, Aiden whipped his off in half a second. Sage was a little slower, giving him a much-too-tempting vision of her blindfolded.

"All-expenses-paid engagement celebration for two. The hotel, champagne and room service are on us," Gary said, grinning from the door as he dangled the key. "We'll be back to get you tomorrow night."

"There are toiletries and, um, you know, stuff, in the bathroom," Cailley called over his shoulder. If the wicked laughter from the peanut gallery was any indication, the *stuff* should be interesting.

And play havoc on Aiden's rule number four.

"Don't do anything I wouldn't do," Gary warned before closing the door on the heckling crowd.

And just like that, they were alone.

Aiden looked at Sage, whose expression was somewhere between amused and shell-shocked.

"Should we save these?" Sage asked with a breathless laugh, waving their blindfolds in the air. "Maybe play a little naughty game later?"

Aiden ignored her. Harder to ignore was the image of Sage, naked, blindfolded and tied to that huge bed.

Control, Masters. You're a strong man, keep it in check. The warning didn't seem to go beyond his brain, though. His body was definitely ignoring it.

"Did you know they were planning this?" he asked, watching her face carefully.

"I knew they were up to something, but I figured they were planning a naughty bridal shower or something. You know, with male strippers, lingerie and bar-hopping in a limo." She looked around the room, her expression a study in amused delight. "But can you believe this? It's like pretty awesome, isn't it?"

"It's a regular sex-fest," he said, his gaze not shifting. He'd seen enough when they walked in—or were hauled in, rather. Besides the stuff Cailley had mentioned, there was champagne on ice, a tray of fruit, a variety of body oils and what looked like hot fudge. He'd have to check the closet for sex toys and leather.

"Well, then," he mused, moving to the window to shift the curtains and check if their friends had left. "This should be interesting."

It wasn't that far of a walk back to town. But the possibility of being spotted was high, and Sage's flimsy sandals were hardly conducive to a five-mile hike at night.

He had enough cash for a cab. But their friends would know if they returned to town. If he knew Gary, the guy had a snitch in the hotel, too.

"Because I'd say we're stuck here until tomorrow," he told her. Puffing out a breath, Aiden dropped onto the couch. It was short, but comfy. He'd slept in worse places.

"Thank you," Sage said quietly, sliding the scarf back and forth between her fingers.

"For?"

"For tonight. For going along. For, you know," she gestured vaguely toward the west and the general direction of her father's house, "for playing devoted fiancé. I know this wasn't easy for you."

"It's not like it was torture to pretend to be engaged to you," he disagreed with a shrug. "Besides, it was actually great hanging out with everyone again. It's been awhile."

He'd forgotten what it was like to be a part of a group that went back, many of them, to kindergarten. The camaraderie, the verbal shorthand, the simple acceptance.

He hadn't realized how tightly he'd been wound the last few years—hell, the last dozen years—until this week, when he'd finally unwound.

He looked at the woman across from him, realizing it was more because of her than anything else that he felt so relaxed. So at peace.

"So, what shall we do for the next thirty or so hours?" Sage mused in a husky voice as she wandered. Her eyes never left his as she skimmed her fingers over the champagne. She took a strawberry from the tray and bit into it, the juice glistening on her lips. When she reached the hot fudge, she dipped one finger in, then sucked it clean.

The image, and the message, damn near killed Aiden.

He wasn't an idiot.

He knew the heat, the attraction and passion between them was incendiary. They could fight it, of course. But Sage clearly didn't want to.

Did he?

He'd come home wondering what the hell mattered in his life. What was real and solid and enduring. Was it just the situation that had him thinking that Sage might be all of that? And if she was, would sex between them make it stronger? Or flat-out destroy it?

He wasn't sure he cared, though.

Not anymore.

EXCITEMENT, NERVES and delight danced a wild jig in Sage's tummy. The evening had been a lot of fun. The champagne she'd drunk earlier was still bubbling, light and happy in her head.

And Aiden was looking at her like he wanted to lick her from lips to toes and back again. Ever since last week when he'd kissed her crazy on his coffee table, she'd been dreaming of seeing that look again.

Wishing.

Hoping.

Planning what she'd do if she saw it, even as she tried to talk herself out of wanting it so much.

And now that it was there, gleaming in his hazel eyes…

She figured it was time to get moving.

"So, I guess this is what they'd call a prehoneymoon practice session," she said, dipping her finger in the hot fudge again and walking over to offer him a taste.

He looked at her, then the fudge, then back at her.

"I didn't poison it," she pointed out, rolling her eyes.

"I'm not hungry."

Oooh. Sage giggled. A challenge.

She loved playing.

"But it's yummy," she said, tapping the cooling chocolate against his lower lip. "Aren't you just a little hungry?"

She stuck her finger into her mouth, swirled her tongue and licked it clean. His pulse jumped in his throat. Yeah, he was hungry.

"It's delicious. Are you sure you're not just a little hungry?" She moved closer, resting her unchocolatey hand against his chest for balance, stepped on tiptoe and licked the chocolate off his lip. "Mmm, yeah. Delicious."

"You're playing with fire," he warned.

"Yummy and hot," she promised.

"This is a bad idea," Aiden said, even as his hands skimmed under her skirt, searching for warmth. She closed her eyes when he found it, moaning softly as he slid his fingers along the wet fabric of her panties.

"It feels good to me," she breathed, kissing her way along the strong angle of his jaw, then skimming her lips down his throat to that sensitive spot at the base of his neck.

A thrill zinged through her when he stiffened.

She loved making him react. Loved even more when that reaction meant things got hard.

"Once we do this, we can't go back," he murmured. As if he wanted to make sure she was completely aware of the consequences, he pulled back. Both his hand from her panties, and his neck from her amazing lips.

Sage sighed, then gave him an impatient look.

She'd been having fun and he was definitely interrupting.

"We're messing with our friendship, Sage. We're changing everything if we do this."

Rarely felt frustration, the kind that teetered right there on the edge of anger, surged through Sage.

Dammit, she was so close. So, so close.

Her orgasm was right there, just out of reach.

And Aiden whose fingers it was dangling from.

She needed this. She needed the delight and the fun and the power of losing herself in sex.

She needed this connection with Aiden. Fake fiancé or not, he was the only person who knew what she was going through.

She got why he was hesitating. She understood the ramifications of their stepping over that line.

It'd change their relationship.

They couldn't go back.

It might impact her father later if they couldn't be in the same room together.

Blah blah blah.

She didn't care.

That was all future stuff. She'd worry about it then.

She wanted to feel good now.

With that in mind, she shifted, moving closer to Aiden and sliding her leg up and down the length of his. The fabric of his slacks against her bare skin was delicious. But nowhere near as delicious as the feel of his hands on her.

She wanted more.

She wanted it all.

And she was going to get it.

"You're so sweet to worry about us," she told him quietly, tracing her finger over his lip and giving him her most appreciative look.

"Sweet. Right."

She took comfort at the pain in his voice. And the steel rod of an erection pressing against her thigh.

"You're the careful one. The planner." When he narrowed his eyes, as if trying to figure out what she was up to, she fluttered her lashes. "I'm the emotional one. The leap-and-forget-to-look one."

"Okay," he said, sounding like he was agreeing, but conditionally.

"But here's what you need to ask yourself. Really, how good of friends were we anyway?" she asked with a teasing smile. "I mean, what are we potentially giving up here? We see each other once every two or three years, we live in totally different parts of the world, and our only tie is my father."

"You're justifying," he warned.

She sighed, a deep breath that thrust her breasts against his chest. It felt so good, his hard muscles against her equally hard nipples. She almost groaned when he shifted away.

Damn him.

He wasn't going to simply let their passion take over.

Nope, he was going to make her justify her position, clarify their situation and agree to some stupid thing that would make him feel like he had an escape hatch.

A part of her wanted to.

She wanted him that much.

But for once, she didn't want to shortchange herself by giving the guy everything and asking for nothing in return. Been there, done that, have the angst-filled past to prove it.

This was Aiden. He knew her. Inside and out.

He either understood and accepted her, including all the baggage this might bring. Or he didn't.

And if he didn't, well, she'd simply have to make him.

Because she was getting that orgasm, dammit.

"Aiden, tell me the truth. A simple yes or no answer will suffice. Or, in your case, one grunt for yes, two for no." She moved back, away from the warm temptation of his body.

It would have been nice if he didn't look so relieved, but hey, she'd take care of that. A couple of buttons and a tug of one bow and, in a slinky swish of fabric, she stood bare, except for her bra and panties. The rich-purple satin and lace cupped her breasts and hugged her hips in a mouth-watering invitation.

His eyes glazed over, and his jaw dropped. Just a tiny bit, but enough to give her ego a lovely boost and her heart an excited leap.

"Aiden?" she prompted.

"What?" he grunted.

"Yes or no?"

He ripped his gaze from her body, and with a deep breath, met her eyes.

"What?" he asked again.

"Yes?" Sage pointed to her body, then using the side of her hand, waved it from chest to thigh.

He audibly swallowed as his eyes followed along.

"Or no?" She pulled her fingers into her palm and used her thumb to gesture over her shoulder to the door and its safe exit.

This time he didn't look where she pointed.

Instead, he looked right into her eyes.

All of a sudden, the game was scary serious.

It was Sage's swallow that echoed through the room now.

Her heart that beat a mile a minute, pounding so hard she was surprised she didn't pass out.

Her body ached with need, but at the same time, her toes twitched with the urge to run.

Because Aiden's face had just gotten serious.

"It's gonna get ugly," he told her, coming nearer. Not touching, but so close she could feel the heat of his body wrapping around her.

"Sex between us is going to be ugly?" she asked, her hands lifting in front of his chest. Following his lead, she didn't touch. Just ran them along his body as if she were testing his energy field.

"Sex between us is going to be mind-blowing," he said, his words low. His eyes were like fire, so hot and tempting as they looked into hers. "It's going to be so good, you'll never forget it. You'll never get over it. It's going to be addicting sex. Make-you-come-in-ten-years-just-at-the-memory-of-it sex."

"Oh, my," Sage whimpered. She had to press her thighs tightly together, they were trembling so much. The move squeezed the swollen folds of her throbbing clitoris, sending shivers of delight through her body.

"It's going to be that good," he promised, his hand skimming over her hair. Light as a whisper, but she felt his touch through her entire being.

"And the messy part?"

"When this engagement is over, so is all that great sex," he told her.

And there it was. His escape hatch.

Sage considered telling him no. That she wasn't willing to limit things to just *this* moment. That if something incredible happened, if magic sparked between them, she wanted to be able to pursue it.

But if she did, he'd take his heat and leave.

So she did the smartest thing she could.

She wrapped her arms around his neck, pressed her body tight against his and took his mouth with all of the need, all of the passion and desire inside her.

And dared him to resist.

8

AIDEN CONSIDERED HIMSELF a very smart man. Not one who often gave in to impulse. Decisions—especially big ones—required careful thought, strategic planning and a vigilant consideration of all possible outcomes.

Ignoring any of that often led to mistakes.

Even regrets.

Intellectually, he knew this was exactly that. One of those impulsive mistakes that would lead to regrets.

But intellect took a backseat to the pounding desire and the clawing, aching need engulfing his body right now.

His mouth moved over Sage's. She was so soft. So damned sweet. The rich intensity of chocolate coated her lips, but the addicting flavor was all Sage. His tongue delved deep, but he knew he'd never get enough.

Not of tasting her.

Not of touching her.

His hands skimmed, featherlight, over her shoulders. Her skin was so soft, a vivid contrast against the lace of her bra. He cupped his palm over her full breast, groaning at the feel of her as her flesh filled his hand.

She whimpered, a tiny mewling sound that echoed through his head. She scraped her nails down his biceps, curving her fingers over the hard muscles and making another sound—this one appreciation—that made Aiden want to flex and give thanks for the intensive SEAL PT he went through on a daily basis.

"You have the most incredible body," she whispered, her hands roaming his chest now. "I could spend hours worshipping it."

"Babe, I was thinking the exact same thing." To prove it, he skimmed one hand down the gentle curve of her spine before sliding it back up and unsnapping her bra. A flick of one finger, then another over the straps and he felt it ripple between their bodies on the way to the floor.

"You're so hard," she breathed, pressing open-mouthed kisses along his shoulder as her hands roamed his biceps again. "Hard, delicious muscles."

"You're so soft," he countered, his fingers tracing the delicate coral areola of one full breast before he rubbed his thumb over her nipple. It hardened gratifyingly fast, pebbling against his thumb, making him groan.

"Hard, solid shoulders," she murmured, her hands pressing, flat-palmed, over his shoulders before sweeping down his chest. She curved her fingers, scraping her nails over his nipples on her way down, then again on the trip back up.

"Soft, delicate breasts," he breathed, cupping both in his hands, his thumbs working the nipples as he weighed the tantalizing globes.

Needing more, he lowered his head to sip at one nipple, then the other. So as not to leave either feeling bereft, he worked one with his mouth while his thumb teased the other. Teeth scraped, his tongue laved. The already hard nubbins sharpened into rock-hard pebbles of desire.

Sage's fingers clenched and unclenched, digging into

his waist now as her breath quickened. Her hips squirmed as she tried to move closer.

As if she couldn't stand the barrier, she pushed his shirt away, forcing him to let go of his bounty long enough to get his arms free of the sleeves. She fumbled with his belt, her hands rubbing over his rock-hard erection as she tried to free him.

She was driving him crazy.

Being an equal-opportunity lover, he figured it was only fair to drive her crazy, too. A task he took quite seriously.

He skimmed his fingers along the elastic of her panties. It only took a push to send them sliding down her legs.

"I'm naked," she noted.

"Mmm," he agreed, stepping back to get a good look.

Sweet baby, she was gorgeous.

Long, lithe, golden and gorgeous.

"You're still fully clothed," she pointed out.

"This a problem?"

"I can't do naughty things to you until we're in an equal state of undress." She tilted her chin, giving him a haughty look at odds with her naked glory.

"What kind of naughty things?"

"The kind that involve my tongue."

Aiden was pretty sure he set a new personal record for stripping naked.

"And look," Sage said, holding up a glass bowl filled with condoms. "Wasn't it sweet of our friends to take such good care of us."

"Great. Gimme," he told her with a grin, bending his fingers in a c'mere gesture.

"You'd be the expert on protection," Sage murmured, giving him the bowl. "Bet I can show you something new, though."

"Go for it," he suggested, handing a condom right back to her.

Her eyes twinkling, Sage arched one brow, then used her teeth to rip the foil open.

She didn't pull out the condom, just held it high in one hand while she reached the other around the back of his neck to pull his mouth down.

Tongues dueling, the kiss went from hot to incendiary with the nip of her teeth.

Before it got really good, though, she moved. Her mouth as hot as her body, she kissed her way down his throat, over his chest. Her tongue swirled around his nipples, making Aiden groan and grip her waist.

Then she slid out of his grasp, and down his body.

"Sage," he said quietly, not sure he could take much more.

Her lips wrapped around the sensitive tip of his penis.

Yeah. He'd take more. As much as she wanted to give.

She sipped at his head, her eyes locking on his as she swirled her tongue around and around. It was like being stroked in wet velvet.

He used to be a civilized guy. A decorated member of the United States Armed Forces. A brilliant mind.

Now, Sage naked at his feet and his body pounding with need, he was a savage.

"Bed," he growled.

"Here," she challenged, quickly sliding the latex over his erection.

Never one to refuse a dare, he grabbed her arms, swept her up the length of his body. With a wicked grin, she slid one foot along the back of his thigh until she reached his waist. Aiden gripped her by the hips, hefting her high. She wrapped her other leg so she was straddling him.

Aiden braced himself, digging his heels into the carpet. Fingers digging into her butt, he angled and thrust.

"Oh, my God," she gasped, her hands tight on his shoulders. "You're like Super Lover. With special powers and everything."

"Babe, you don't know the half of it," he told her, his ego swelling even bigger than his rock-hard erection.

Guiding her, sliding her, he tried to pace himself.

She was so hot. So tight.

Her breasts slid over his chest, her nipples leaving fiery trails on his skin.

His fingers dug into her butt. He closed his eyes, forcing himself to disconnect, to grab those last feeble threads of control.

"Wait," he demanded, stilling.

"Noooo," she moaned.

"Patience, Sage," he ordered on a growl.

Still buried inside her, it took him two steps to reach the bed. It took three seconds to calculate the odds of them both hitting the mattress with him still inside her, and his dick not snapping off.

Deciding they weren't really in his favor, he took her mouth in a hot, wet kiss as he slowly, reluctantly pulled out.

Her protest was half moan, half whimper.

Still holding her, he carefully, as if she were precious treasure, laid her on the edge of the bed.

His eyes met hers.

She was so damned beautiful.

He slid into her wet heat, her body gripping him so tight he almost cried with the intensity of the pleasure.

This, he realized as he plunged, was home.

He'd finally come home.

The thought exploded, bigger than the orgasm building, like an emotional climax spewing all over the place.

He pushed it aside, focusing on his body. On the building pleasure.

On giving the same pleasure to Sage.

He plunged, slow and deep. Each thrust met by her hips, their sweat-slick bodies moving in sync with each other.

Her breath came faster with each descent.

A soft, silken flush washed over her chest, coating her breasts a tempting shade of strawberry. He had to taste.

Arms locked, he leaned down, swiping his tongue over her nipple.

Sage cried out, arching higher, offering her breast for his feasting pleasure.

Who was he to say no?

Aiden feasted away.

Thrusting deep, he sucked on her nipple.

Then with a balance honed by years of physical training, he straightened and shifted his weight onto one hand. Still thrusting, he reached between their bodies to find her swollen bud.

She shuddered, her eyes flying open to meet his.

The passion in her gaze was an erotic invitation, begging him to do more, to make her feel every possible delight. Winding tighter and tighter inside, like a bomb about to explode, his body tensed.

"Go," he ordered through clenched teeth.

"Make me," she challenged.

The climax throbbed, right there on the edge. Determined to send her over first, Aiden pulled out until just the tip of his dick was buried in her warmth.

Her brow creased, a look of frustration flashing in her eyes.

He plunged again, slow and intense until he was buried so deep he wasn't sure where she started and he left off.

Her eyes widened, frustration gone and passion fogging the aquamarine depths.

He slid back out.

She whimpered.

He plunged, a little faster this time.

Her breath came in pants now.

In. Out.

Faster and faster.

Her fingers skewered his butt, her hips thrusting to meet his. Slamming tighter and tighter against each other. Aiden growled.

"Go," he demanded again.

"Yessssss."

She went over with a gasp, her body arching high, pressing tight against his. Her breath coming in panting whimpers now, she ground her pelvis against him as if she were trying to milk every last drop of delight from his body.

It was the look in her misty eyes that sent him over. Hazy passion, dancing joy and absolute trust. Balanced on her shoulder blades, she reached up to cup her hands over his cheeks, pulling his face close for a sweet kiss.

The sweetness was his undoing.

Aiden exploded.

His body. His mind.

His heart.

Every piece of him blew to bits as he lost himself in her body. He lost track of time. Black edged his vision but he never lost sight of her face. Of those eyes.

He loved her.

Dammit.

THIS WAS IT. Sage sank into the delight, floating on a cloud of pleasure so deep and intense, she felt as though it'd taken over her body.

She'd finally found it.

Bliss.

That elusive answer to everything she'd spent her life searching for. The key to everything she wanted, everything she needed.

Aiden was her bliss.

Her bliss rolled off her, pressing a warm kiss against her shoulder as he moved away for a second. Then, before she could react to his moving—or her discovery—he was back, sweeping her into his arms. Again.

Before she even registered that she was up, he lay her down again, this time at the top of the bed, where he joined her, pulling the blankets over them both.

He was such a prince.

The Prince of Bliss.

Her eyes flew open and she slammed down to earth as the pleasure cloud evaporated in a puff of panic.

Oh, shit.

No. Oh, no, no, no.

Not Aiden.

He couldn't be her bliss.

It was just the sex talking.

Her cognitive skills were fogged by waves of orgasmic pleasure.

Her brain was high on sugar from that fingerful of hot fudge.

It was a mentally lethal combination.

Besides, the guy had some serious skills in bed. Aiden. A guy she'd known for most of her life, was the world's greatest lover.

The possessor of the magical key to bliss.

She was in so much trouble.

"Sage?"

She pulled the bedspread higher, tucking it under her chin. Hey, she considered it a victory that it wasn't over her head.

"Sage?" he repeated when she didn't respond. "Are you okay?"

Was she okay? Her mind raced.

She could run, get the hell out of here and escape. The room, the town, the state.

But her dad needed her.

And she'd promised Aiden that she was in it for the long haul. She might be a flake, but she didn't break her promises.

She could tell him how she felt.

He was a SEAL. He could handle the terror.

Or she could do what she did best.

Revel in the moment, enjoy every blissful second of what they had here, and deal with the fallout later.

"You okay?"

"I'm amazing," she stated.

"Yeah, you are," he agreed with a satisfied sound that was half growl, half sigh.

He sounded so sexy. Pure satisfied masculinity. She'd done that, made him growl with pleasure.

She wanted to do it again.

With a deep breath, she shoved back the fear and grabbed onto the moment as she rolled onto one elbow.

He was gorgeous.

His eyes soft with fading passion, his lips swollen from kissing her. And that body. Oh, yeah, she had a lot to thank Uncle Sam for. Because while nature might have given him a very nice start, the military had honed his physique to a work of art.

A very yummy work of art.

"You know we have the rest of the weekend to fill," she murmured.

"Any ideas?"

"I do think we should use the hot fudge before it's cold," she pointed out.

Disappointment flashed in his eyes for a second, then faded to friendly concern.

"You're hungry?"

"I am," she said with a nod.

As much because she needed to move as to add some fun to their sexy times, Sage scurried from the bed. Comfortably naked, she crossed the room to get the fudge, unplugging the warmer and bringing just the bowl back with her. It wasn't until she reached the side of the bed that she noticed Aiden's expression.

All of a sudden, she felt like a goddess. The worship in his eyes was as hot as his mouth had been earlier.

"Amazing," was all he said, though.

Her cheeks warmed. How silly. Had a guy ever made her blush before? She couldn't remember even once, especially after they'd got naked together. But Aiden, he had a way of making her feel every kind of thing she'd never imagined before.

"I get the first lick," she decided, holding the bowl aloft.

"Nope." He grabbed the bowl with one hand, her wrist with the other. A quick tug had her on the mattress next to him. "You licked earlier. Now it's my turn."

"Oh, my." She shifted onto her elbows, tossing her hair back to keep it out of the sticky range.

"You didn't bring a spoon?" he asked, giving the bowl a confused look.

Sage's lips twitched. He was so cute.

"I'd planned to use my fingers," she told him.

He frowned, then as if realizing the silliness of worrying about utensils when his plate was her body, he grinned back.

"Dessert time, then," he announced, dipping two fingers into the thick brown sweet. He paused as if testing the temperature, then gave her a long look. Like an artist assessing a blank canvas, trying to decide where to start worshipping his masterpiece.

He must have decided he was a top-down kind of guy, because he took that scoop of chocolate and swirled it around one nipple, then the other.

He gave her a wicked look, then dipped his fingers again and painted a smile on her tummy.

"Happy," he said with a grin.

"Indeed?"

"Yeah. I'll prove it."

He offered her his chocolate-coated fingers. More than ready to enjoy, Sage sucked the chocolate off of them one at a time. His dick danced a hard tribute of delight as she did.

"Yum," she told him.

"Let's see."

He proceeded to lick her body clean.

Sage was hot and wet by the time he finished licking the smile clean. As he licked, his own fingers worked their way between her thighs, sliding inside her to swirl, then plunge, then swirl again.

"Aiden," she begged, her fingers digging into the mattress.

"Just a sec, I'm eating," he told her as he shifted lower, his shoulders pressing her thighs wider.

He moved his fingers to make room for his tongue.

Still sipping, his groan of delight making it clear he found her as tasty as the chocolate, he sucked and licked until Sage exploded.

Lights flashed behind her eyes.

The rich scent of chocolate filled her senses.

Her body trembled as he kissed his way back up, burying his face in her throat before taking her mouth with his.

His hands felt so good on her body. Strong, firm, delicious. When he touched her, she was in heaven.

His hands made her feel sexy. Gave her the most intense pleasure. At the same time, she felt safe. Like nothing could hurt her when he was around.

"Chocolate bliss," she said, licking her bottom lip.

"Sage bliss," he corrected, rubbing his thumb over the corner of her mouth. "Delicious."

Before she could claim her turn, he sank into a mindblowing kiss. His mouth molded hers, his tongue sweeping inside with the richly addicting taste of fudge.

She wanted to eat him up.

To keep him, forever.

Afraid of that thought, she moved fast, shifting so she was over his body. She ran her hands over his mouthwatering expanse of muscles, then straddled his hips.

"Yum," he growled, his hands cupping her breasts. "I like the view."

"You're going to like the ride even more," she promised.

Teasing them both, she leaned across him to grab a condom from the bowl on the nightstand. The move brushed her breast over his face. As she straightened, she brushed over him again, but slower this time.

A clever, resourceful kind of guy, he took good advantage of her offer, sipping at her nipple. It felt so good she had to stay for a few extra seconds to enjoy. Desire wound, tense and edgy in her belly again. You'd think she'd be sated, or at least comfortable. Instead, she was as needy and desperate for Aiden as she'd been earlier.

He nipped, then laved her nipple as if soothing the wound. Her thighs quivered and the desire coiled tighter. Even tighter than earlier, she realized. Now that she'd had him, now that she knew how incredible it was, she was even more turned on.

And in very real danger of coming right here and now.

"Not yet," she said to both of them, straightening so quickly that his mouth made a slurping sound. "I've got plans here, sexy boy. You're not going to distract me."

"Bet I could."

Shifting down his thighs a little, she tore open the condom and gave him a wicked look.

"I'll bet you could, too. But think of everything you'd miss out on if you do."

To give him an idea of what that everything included, she shifted again, poised above his erection. She bent her knees just a little, so the tip of his dick was right there, at the entrance of delight.

Her eyes locked on his, she trailed her fingers up her thighs, along the sides of her waist. She paused to cup her own breasts, loving how his eyes darkened and he groaned.

As soon as he reached out, his hands replacing hers, she continued her journey. Her fingers skimmed the sides of her throat, then she combed them through her hair.

She arched her back and lowered her body at the same time.

Taking him inside her.

Shuddering as he filled her with his hard length.

Her inner walls trembled around him, clenching in so so many tiny orgasms.

Her breath sped up.

Her heart pounded so hard, she could barely hear their breaths over the beating in her head.

His thumbs rubbed her nipples in time with her moves.

Up and down.

Around and around.

He was so good.

So delicious.

And so incredible to watch.

His eyes glazed over.

His body tensed beneath her, those gorgeous muscles rippling as he moved. His hips lifted now to meet hers. Their bodies came together faster. But his hands never left her breasts, his focus never left her face.

She'd always dreamed of bliss. Of finding that perfect something that touched her heart, filled her world with joy. With this feeling, she could do anything. Be everything.

As good as she was at dreaming, at vividly imagining what bliss would be like, she'd been totally clueless.

This was so much more than she'd ever imagined.

It was bigger.

Brighter.

Totally soul-encompassing.

But even as she sank again into the blissful sexual haze, she could feel the terror hanging there, right over her shoulder like a grim specter, tapping its foot and waiting to engulf her.

9

WHO KNEW GREAT SEX could work up such an appetite? Sage helped herself to a second apple pancake and scooped more eggs onto her plate. Mrs. Green had outdone herself with breakfast today.

"Are you seriously going to eat all of that?" Nina asked, seated across from Sage at the Professor's table. Her plate looked a little sad with its three pieces of fruit and dollop of yogurt.

"I'm hungry," Sage said before taking a huge bite. As soon as she swallowed, she added, "Besides, I have a great metabolism. I'll work this off before dinner."

"Sure you will. If you're having sex with Aiden again."

Unfazed, Sage just smiled and ate a big bite of apple-enriched pancake. Who was she to deny the awesomeness that was her current sex life? Her fork halfway to her mouth, she paused to sigh in appreciation at the memories. Not just of last weekend and their engagement party after-party, but of the three days following. Lunchtime sex. Poolside sex. Dragging-her-along-for-a-run-and-her-distracting-him sex.

That was a lot of sex.

She'd had more awesome sex in the last five days than she'd had mediocre sex the entire rest of her life.

Sage ran her tongue over her bottom lip, reveling in the taste of warm cinnamon and hot thoughts.

Oh, yeah. Her metabolism was working overtime.

As were her imagination, her optimism and her libido.

She couldn't have dreamed up a better distraction from worrying about her father if she'd tried.

Or a better way to enjoy Mrs. Green's fabulous cooking.

"I don't think I've ever seen you like this," Nina observed, sneaking a piece of pancake off Sage's plate.

"Hungry? Or sexually satisfied?" Sage asked with a wink.

"Content."

Whoa.

Sage frowned, slowly lowering her fork to the plate.

"Content? That's a funny way to describe me." Satisfied, giddy, worried, confused. Those she could see. But content?

Her frown deepened. Had she ever been content? Why was she just now realizing it was something she might want?

"Probably because you've never been described that way before." Nina laughed. "From preschool on, you've always been off searching for something. A different toy, better crayons, another adventure. I think this is the first time I've ever seen you seem satisfied with where you were at. With what you have."

Content? Satisfied?

Was that what this feeling was? Sage took a deep breath, pushing her plate away. Suddenly, she wasn't so hungry.

"What's wrong?" Nina asked.

"I don't know." What was wrong?

She wanted to be content. To find satisfaction. To live a happy life. This was as close to bliss as she'd ever been.

Nina was right. She was always searching for something. For someone. For that magical connection that would make her feel whole.

"Are you getting cold feet?" Nina asked, pulling Sage's half-eaten pancakes toward her to take a bite. "That's normal, you know."

More like suddenly realizing that she'd spent most of her life on a quest, without a clue what she actually wanted. Home? The idea of staying in one place, always, was boring. A person? She'd thought that—and been wrong—often enough to know that happiness had to come from within first.

"Did you get cold feet before you married Jeffrey?" she asked. Maybe she was so upside down, her cold feet manifested as contentment.

"Sure did," Nina said around a big mouthful.

"What'd you do?"

"Eloped." Washing the pancake down with a sip of juice, Nina shrugged. "I knew I'd screw it up if I kept worrying. There are a million questions that go with a wedding. Color schemes, flower choices, menus and guest lists. Even when you think you know what you want, it's still crazy."

"So you eloped to avoid the wedding decisions?"

"Sort of." Nina wrinkled her nose, then gave in and ate another bite of pancake. "But mostly it was to escape all the second thoughts. I mean, I knew Jeffrey and I were perfect for each other. But it was like all the wedding questions sparked marriage questions. Silly doubts, crazy worries."

"I guess it's a good thing I'm not planning my wedding yet, then," Sage said, suddenly sad *and* confused.

"That doesn't mean you're not getting cold feet. Are you thinking that the two of you are crazy happy right now?"

"We are happy," Sage agreed slowly. At least she was.

Other than her worries over her father, the last few weeks were about the happiest she could remember having.

"Are you wondering how that happy can last? Like, maybe this is the peak and it's got to all be downhill from here?"

"I don't want to answer that," Sage muttered.

"You're figuring the sex is wild, he treats you like a princess and you both are in basic agreement about everything, right?" Nina waited for Sage's reluctant shrug before patting her hand and continuing. "But there's no way that can last. So you're worried. Even while you fall asleep in his arms with a huge, satisfied smile on your face, you're trying to memorize the moment because you figure it's all gonna be gone."

Sage tapped her fingernail against her plate a few times, took a deep breath, then shook her head.

"You know, I'd really appreciate it if you'd stay the hell out of my head. Friends should let friends enjoy their freak-outs in peace."

She laughed along with Nina as if it were all a fun joke. But inside, Sage wondered if she'd become a cliché.

This was a fake engagement, with a definite ending that wouldn't include rings or growing old together or baby names. No ties, no fears, no big boogeyman future to worry about. Just great sex between good friends.

"So?"

"So, what?" Sage asked.

"Cold feet?"

"Yeah," Sage admitted with a sigh. "Total cold feet."

Not about her fake engagement, though.

Nope. She had cold feet about her entire life.

THREE HOURS LATER, she was cozied up in her favorite window seat in her father's study, staring at her sock-covered feet and wondering what it'd take to warm them back up. Her laptop was on the table next to her, a bowl of M&M's—red only, today—nearby.

"Sage, darling."

"Hello, Daddy-o." Sage greeted him, looking up from her laptop. A quick search of his features and her shoulders relaxed. He looked good. Really, really good. "You're back from the hospital early."

"What're you working on?" he asked, settling into his plush easy chair and giving her an expectant look.

"How do you know I'm working on anything?" she asked, offering him the bowl of candy.

He took a handful, then held up one piece of candy-coated chocolate.

"Red. Energy, right? You always eat red M&M's when you're working on a piece you plan to sell."

"You know me so well," she said with a laugh.

"I do, I do," he agreed. "And your momma used to eat hers the same way."

Sage smiled, always thrilled to hear that she was, in any way, like the mother she'd lost so young.

"Did she teach me to separate them, then?"

"And to designate colors for moods. Yellow for happy, blue for sad."

"I always think of blue for peace," she admitted. "It's easier to ignore the sad."

He gave her a long, intense look that made her want to squirm.

"You're distracting yourself," he observed quietly. "Trying to do as many things as you can to keep from thinking about what might happen to me."

Do Aiden as many times as she could, was more like it.

Sage swallowed, trying to ease the sudden tightness in

her throat. She glanced at her fingers, aglitter with rings and twined together in a nervous knot.

"I don't want to talk about it," she said quietly, finally looking up to meet her father's eyes. "Words have power. If we don't discuss it, it'll have less power. Over me, over the outcome. Over my emotions."

He gave her one of his patented calm looks. The ones that said he had all the time in the world to wait until she got the problem figured out. He'd worn that expression when she was learning to tie her shoes, learning to drive, talking about boys, recovering from her first hangover. Heck, she was pretty sure he'd worn that look for at least half the days in her life.

That's what made him so awesome.

She blinked fast, knowing tears weren't going to help either of them.

"I know, that's too new-agey for you." She wrinkled her nose and shrugged. "But I'm just not ready to talk about it."

Hopefully she wouldn't have to be. He seemed better. He was responding well to treatment. Maybe he'd get through this and they'd never have to talk about it at all.

After a long consideration, her father nodded. He looked a little relieved, too, she noted. So, there. She'd just made them both feel a little better.

The tight ball of dread didn't shift from her belly. It'd been there for two weeks now and she was getting used to it. At least, she was telling herself that. And like not talking about the bad stuff, she figured if she told herself that often enough, she'd eventually believe it.

"Then let's talk about happier subjects, shall we?" her father suggested, folding both hands over his belly in lecture mode.

Sage automatically straightened, shoulders back and chin up, ready to listen.

"Let's discuss your future. I'm quite pleased thinking about it," he told her, his smile backing up his claim.

"My future?"

As in, her and Aiden. Together forever in wedded bliss. Was that the future he meant?

Was today future day or something? They all had their pretty label, why couldn't it be left at that?

Then she saw the look in her father's eyes.

That was more than patience.

That was stubbornness.

The same stubbornness she saw in the mirror on a regular basis.

Nerves bounced so hard in her belly, they almost tossed her breakfast right back out her mouth.

Holy crap.

Was he going to talk about babies? Buying a house? Saving for college, retirement plans and oh, God, her getting a *real* job?

She swallowed hard, pressed a hand to her belly in warning and tried to smile.

Maybe it'd be easier if she got over herself and they talked about his health.

"Yes, dear. Your future. You and Aiden are going to get married. That means you might want to consider some changes."

Oh, man.

Changes?

She loved changing things.

Her hairstyle. Her address. Her job. Her view.

But only when she was ready. On her whim, when the muse called, when she was bored.

"What kind of changes?" she asked tentatively, afraid to deny him anything.

"You're going to be building a life together, you and Aiden. Considering your future. Now, I'm not saying you should live here, although Villa Rosa is a lovely town to raise a family," he said, chuckling. He looked past her shoulder, casting an affectionate smile out the window at the distant view of the town.

She couldn't quite smile back. Not with all those words swirling through her head. A family? The future?

"Shouldn't Aiden be here for this chat?" she asked. He was trained to deal with scary stuff.

"No, no. I'm sure we'll have many a chat, all three of us. But right now I just wanted to talk to you."

Surprise shooed away some of the nerves in Sage's stomach.

He'd rather talk to her than Aiden? She'd never felt slighted or overlooked in her father's relationship with Aiden. Her place in her father's life and his heart was secure and firm. But, still, this talk was about Aiden. Why wouldn't her father want him included?

"Don't you think that soon, after the two of you set the wedding date and make your decisions about settling down, that perhaps it'll be time for some career changes?" the Professor asked, his smile in place and that bulldog look in his eyes.

Sage squinted, glancing at her laptop and its waiting article, then back at her father.

"I really don't think I'm a career kind of person, Dad. I mean, I like writing my blog posts and stirring up attention. There are a lot of things that deserve that focus, after all. And the posts, the articles I sell, they are great. But that's more of a hobby than a career." She nibbled at her bottom lip, her fingers pleating the fabric of her skirt and she considered her last three or four jobs. "I didn't much like retail, and while I'm a good barista, there's only so much coffee I want to serve, you know?"

She waited, wondering if he had a new job or career

option he wanted to suggest for her to try. Maybe something with flowers or outdoors. She just might like working with nature.

"I meant Aiden's career, dear."

"Oh."

Ahhhh.

Sage blew out a long breath.

That's why Aiden wasn't included in this particular conversation.

"You mean Aiden being a SEAL? You're worried about the danger?"

"Aren't you?"

Sage opened her mouth, then closed it. She should be, shouldn't she? She blinked a few times, trying to figure out why she wasn't. Finally, she shrugged.

"No. I'm really not. I'm not oblivious to the dangers, but Aiden's served in wartime and come through fine. I mean, he has a few scars here and there. And sure, his shoulder seems to ache a little when he first wakes up. But that's the kind of thing any guy who's led an active life would face."

"It's not quite the same as if he were playing weekends sports or putting in his forty hours a week on his feet, Sage. He's jumping out of airplanes, diving under the sea, chasing down wrongdoers and operating under enemy fire."

And all of that, except the enemy fire part, sounded wildly exciting. But clearly not to her father.

"I know," she agreed quietly. "He's an elite warrior. But that's the thing, Dad. He's been through some of the most intensive training there is. On top of that, he's smart and careful."

"Is that enough for you? Will that be enough to tell your children when their father is always gone? Gone, and you can't tell them where?"

No. No, no, no. It was all Sage could do not to press

her hands over her ears. Enough with the children talk. She felt safer thinking about Aiden jumping out of an airplane under enemy fire into the ocean than she did thinking about herself raising kids. As flaky as everyone said she was? She was positive Aiden was definitely better at being a SEAL than she'd be at being a parent.

"Dad, that's way, way in the future. Why don't we just get through Aiden's leave, our engagement? You know, celebrate now instead of worrying about tomorrow." Her toes twitched with the need to hit the floor and scurry out of the room. But she managed to keep her smile calm and cheerful.

The name of the game was making her dad feel good, she reminded herself.

"I know you'd rather not think about the future, Sage. I'm not advising you make plans and act on them today. I'm simply suggesting you begin considering your future. Thinking about what you might like it to be."

"I'm great at dreaming," she assured him, leaning forward to pat his hand. "I'll definitely be thinking about the what-ifs and possibilities."

There.

A comforting sort of vow that promised nothing. Her specialty. One that had always worked wonderfully in the past in answer to everything from her travel plans to her college plans.

"Ah, yes, you are a dreamer," he agreed with a smile of his own. Noting the look in his eyes, Sage sighed. She leaned back against the wall and waited. Lecture, life lesson or well-thought-out suggestion. One of them was heading her way. Or, since he was looking particularly chipper, probably all three.

"I suppose you're spending a lot of time dreaming about your future right now," he pondered, crossing one knee over the other and wrapping his hands around it with a look of contemplation. "Not wedding contemplation, although I understand that's a normal preoccupation for young engaged women."

"The wedding is a ways away," Sage reminded him, flicking her fingers as if shooing the calendar off her radar. "And I'm hardly the big-traditional-wedding type, Dad. It's more likely that we'd send you a plane ticket to meet us on a beach for a sunset ceremony at the last second."

She'd be wearing a sarong, with white flowers in her hair. Aiden would probably insist on wearing his dress uniform, but she was hoping she could convince him to go barefoot with it. After all, the soft white sand would feel so good on his toes.

"Just give me twenty-four hours' notice, more if the trip requires inoculations," he advised with a warm smile. "And since you clearly have that figured out, why don't we discuss what happens after the wedding."

Oh, God. Sage's stomach dove into her toes and her pancakes curdled. Please, no. Not a wedding night chat.

"Where will you spend your marriage?"

She squinted. This wasn't another wedding night chat angle, was it?

"You're not going to want to bounce from station to station, are you? Waiting around, unable to actually see your husband because he's off on a covert operation or dangerous top-secret mission?"

"Sure, why not? It's not like I'll be twiddling my thumbs or staring forlorn out a window." Seeing the concern on his face, she searched her mind for something that might settle his mind. Oh, she had it. "I've got plenty of things to do myself. Actually, I just got an offer to expand some of my blog posts into a series of articles. The publisher has suggested I become a regular columnist for not only their online, but three of their print publications."

"That sounds like a big commitment for you."

Which was why she agreed to no more than a test period. She figured if in four months she wasn't bored, burned out or disenchanted, she'd take their offer.

"Still, what are the odds of marriage success between two people who see so little of each other?"

"I'm not a settle-in-suburbia kind of girl. If I had to live in a nine-to-five existence, I'd go crazy. So for two people like Aiden and me? I'd say the odds are pretty good."

If they were really engaged and in love enough to get married, of course. She ignored the ache in her heart and tried a cheery smile.

"For the short term, maybe. But long term? Don't you think you'd do better if the two of you moved back to Villa Rosa? Here, Aiden can finish his degree, teach at the university. He can finally do justice to that brilliant mind of his."

"I don't think that's what he wants to do, though."

"But married life isn't about what each individual wants for him, or herself, dear. It's about the whole. Society is built on compromise and the greater good."

"You might want to let the politicians know that," she said with a teasing smile.

When he didn't smile back, she let her lips droop again.

So much for a distracting clever subject change.

"Aiden is a brilliant man. I'm sure he realizes that marriage requires changes. And he loves you, dear, so he's going to want to ensure that those changes make you, both of you, happy."

"Uh-huh."

"He just needs to know what you want, so he can begin making it happen." Her father paused, the look on his face pure avuncular pride. She had no idea what she'd done to earn it, but for the first time in her life, it scared the hell out of her.

"But what if that's not what I want?" she asked quietly, terrified that she actually might. How could she want a settled, boring, average life after years of chasing adventure and bliss?

"Think about your future together, about children. There's so much for the two of you to experience. Wouldn't it be better if you experienced it together?" Her father paused, then patted her hand. "Just think about it, darling."

"Of course," Sage promised, setting her bowl down and pushing her laptop away. Suddenly she wasn't so hungry. Or interested in writing a brilliant and fun article that might cement her future.

"Dude, you're insane," Gary panted, huffing as he tried to keep pace with Aiden.

"You didn't have to come along."

"Since you've spent the last week in bed with your fiancée, this was the first shot I had to talk to you. If I'd realized you were insane, I'd have waited until you were through."

Not at all winded, Aiden easily laughed and slowed his pace to nudge Gary with his shoulder.

"I told you it was a ten-mile run. You said you do that three days a week. So what's the problem?"

"I do it on the treadmill, in the air-conditioned gym, with the news on TV to distract me," Gary muttered between huffs.

Aiden laughed again.

It was probably that week in bed Gary had mentioned, but Aiden couldn't ever remember feeling this good.

Alive, energized.

Happy.

Running along a side road that was mostly dirt, while row after row of grapes lined up like good little soldiers in the fields beyond. Gold and green met the blue of the sky, a brilliant backdrop to a fabulous morning run.

He'd missed this.

He was relaxed here. For the first time, Aiden realized how much tension he always set aside when he came to Villa Rosa. Not because he didn't have concerns or responsibilities, but because they were different here.

And the ones he had, they were shared.

By the town. By his friends. By Sage and the Professor.

This was the feeling, he realized, of being home.

Where he knew every tree and side road, not because he'd studied and memorized topographical maps, plotting attack and escape routes. But because he'd walked them hundreds of times. The people might not be his best friends, and he'd never count on most of them in a fight. But they all knew him, and he them. There was something comforting in that.

For a man who hadn't been aware that he needed comfort, it was a weird feeling.

He shot a sideways glance at his running partner. He and Gary had played Little League together. They'd been in the same third-grade class, although Aiden had spent half of his time in the gifted program, and they'd been hard and fast recess buddies. There was a simple camaraderie here with someone he'd known most of his life. An easy acceptance.

His relationships with the other SEALs were tight. Beyond tight, given how hard they worked together, trained together. That they depended on each other for their lives. They were brothers-in-arms. Those relationships were unbreakable.

But they were short-term, too. Teams changed on a regular basis. New assignments, different missions.

"Dude, we gotta stop," Gary panted.

"Why?"

Gary pointed to the little girl on the corner of a private vineyard. Set back a ways from the street, and in clear view of the house behind, she'd placed a slab of wood over two wine barrels and hung a sign.

"We need lemonade," Gary huffed. "Desperately. Have to have it."

"Drinking in the middle of a run isn't a good idea."

"That's my niece. She's saving up to buy a pony," Gary said, nodding toward the little girl again. "C'mon. You can help a ten-year-old out, can't you?"

What were a few potential cramps in the face of a ten-year-old and her pony?

A few minutes, two lemonades and a promise to visit said pony later, and Aiden was halfway in love.

"She's a pistol," he told Gary, watching the kid juggle lemons as a floor show.

"Yeah. She's the image of Darla, my sister. But she's got her dad's personality. You ever imagine what your kid's gonna be like? You? Or Sage?"

"Me or..."

Holy shit.

The idea of a kid—with Sage—suddenly terrified Aiden like no mission, terrorist threat or deadly night maneuver ever had.

"I've gotta finish my run," Aiden said, tossing the cup in the little trash can and giving the pigtailed entrepreneur a smile. "You with me?"

Gary peered up the road, then eyed the house behind his niece. He hung his head and heaved a sigh before giving Aiden a rueful look.

"You kicked my, um, rear, buddy. I'm gonna go see what my sister has for breakfast. Want to join me?"

"I still have six miles to go."

Gary shook his head, thumped Aiden on the back, then waved toward the road.

"Have at it."

Aiden grinned, gave the little girl another smile, then had at it.

He was used to running with others. But there was a kind of peace that came with running alone.

Even if he did feel like he was being chased by Gary's last question.

Him and Sage, having a kid.

What an image.

He didn't know what was more preposterous.

The idea of his life including a kid.

Or of Sage settling down long enough for that to even come into question.

Not that having kids with her wouldn't be fun.

He'd never thought about kids before. But now he grinned a little as he ran, wondering if they'd have his brains and her imagination. Her smile, and zest for life. A boy would be great, but a couple of girls would be fabulous, too.

Even more fun would be the making of said imaginary tots.

Just thinking about that kind of activity with Sage got his heart pumping and quickened his breath in a way that a ten-mile—hell, a fifty-mile—run couldn't.

Especially now that he knew what it was like.

What she was like.

Tasty, imaginative and wild. With so much sweetness, a wicked laugh and a talent for whispering naughty suggestions at just the right time.

Images of their weekend together flashed through his mind, surged through his body. She was amazing. In bed, out of bed.

Just amazing.

Dammit.

Aiden stepped off the road to a patch of grass and dropped to the ground to do fifty push-ups. Gotta send the blood to other muscles. Since he was wearing a pair of navy issue loose gray sweatpants—without a cup— he didn't figure a hard-on was a good accompaniment to his run.

One, two, three…

It didn't matter how great the sex was.

That didn't equate to a future.

Twenty, twenty-one, twenty-two…

And as great as the dream was, he knew it was just that.

A dream.

Built on wishes and thin air, with as much substance as Sage's attention span.

Needing to move, not willing to face the emotions crashing over him at the prospect of giving up a dream he had never admitted he had, he jumped to his feet and started running again. He watched the road in front of him, his running shoes slapping the pavement as if mocking his thoughts.

Here, now, alone in his own mind, he could admit the truth that he'd never share aloud.

He loved Sage. He always had.

He was pretty sure he always would.

She was his fantasy girl, his dream woman.

She was also flighty, flaky and emotional.

Hardly the type of woman who'd make a good military wife. Not that he was interested in a wife. He'd simply paid attention to his friends on the team. First Landon, then Sullivan. Now Lane. They were pairing up like they really believed they could beat the odds stacked against military marriages.

Since that's what SEALs did, beat the odds, Aiden couldn't fault them.

He just knew better than playing the game unless he figured he had as good of a shot.

And Sage? She wasn't marriage material, let alone military-marriage material.

They had now. This crazy, ridiculous fake engagement that was so perfectly Sage. They had to live in the moment, as she'd say.

So he was going to live. And enjoy and revel and bask.

But a future?

A real one?

With Sage?

Not gonna happen.

10

"Why are we doing this again?" Aiden asked, his grumpy tone melting into the warm evening air.

Because she was in desperate need of a distraction?

Because she hadn't been able to get her father's words, or the terror they'd invoked, out of her head or her stomach for three days?

Because maybe an average evening of togetherness with friends would show her how boring this life would be, and she could stop fantasizing about her and Aiden, settling in for their very own happy-ever-after.

He probably didn't want to know any of that, though. So Sage laughed instead, tucking her hand through Aiden's arm and cuddling close as they walked up the path.

"Why are we doing what? Going to dinner at a friend's house? Going together? Or wearing our own underwear instead of each other's?"

"Please." Aiden slanted her a chiding look. "Your thong is too small for me."

"That's because you're sooo big," she drawled, her tone as teasing as the look she gave him in return. He was so fun. She loved this side of him. The relaxed, mellow, not-off-to-fight-secret-battles side.

Maybe her dad was right. Maybe being in Villa Rosa was good for Aiden. Around friends, away from that constant stress and adrenaline overload.

"Seriously. Why the secret dinner plans?"

"Because Nina and her doctor eloped. Cailley and Ana-Maria don't think it's fair that she missed out on all of the torture they disguise as engagement fun, so we're here to plan a little post-marriage excitement."

"That's why you're here. Why am I necessary?"

Since he'd frozen on the bottom porch step, Sage had every reason to believe he'd turn on his heel and leave her to go in alone.

For a woman who'd spent almost all of her adult life going her own way, and whose longest relationship had lasted less months than she had fingers on one hand, going in alone was the norm.

But for the first time, the idea of it made her miserable.

She just wasn't sure if it was the idea of going in alone. Or going without Aiden.

Something to freak out about later, she decided. With all the other freak-outs she was already entertaining. It was getting to be a regular nerve-fest in her brain.

"We need you," she told him with a wide-eyed look, hoping she came across as earnest. "Nina's always been the one to plan these things. According to the other girls, she's the expert and would recognize anything they tried to do. If we're going to surprise her, we need strategy."

"Surprise her with what? A girly shower? One of those underwear parties you women are always talking about?" He gave her a horrified look. "Nope, I'm out."

"What if I promise you naughty sexual favors on the walk home?" she offered.

He gave her his uptight military look. The inscrutable one she figured they taught in SEAL school.

"Fine, I'm in."

Delighted, Sage was still laughing when their host took their jackets. But it wasn't until they were halfway through dessert that it hit her.

This was it.

She'd found her bliss.

Not the settled, suburbia image that her father had painted. That still scared the crap out of her.

But this, here…

Friends, laughter, and a deep feeling of contentment pouring through her. The company was great, and the warm comfort of being back home was always welcome.

She could imagine this same scene, anywhere. With other friends, or friends she hadn't met yet. Different meals, various cities or countries.

Those parts were all interchangeable, all wonderful elements but no one of them was crucial to this feeling inside her heart.

The feeling of joy. Of peace and happiness.

Of love.

It was Aiden that made the difference.

A forkful of molten lava cake halfway to her lips, she stopped and lowered it without tasting to stare at the man next to her.

Engaged in a spirited debate with Gary and Eric over the merits of Chevy versus Ford, he was both animated and relaxed. As if he, too, had found his bliss. Or at least had let go of some of that heaviness he'd been carrying three weeks ago.

This was something she could give him, she realized.

Fun. Laughter and belonging and simple enjoyment.

She wrapped that feeling around her like a soft, warm blanket, cozy and delighted at how fabulous it felt.

The sweetness of it lasted all the way until coffee.

Curled up next to Aiden on the couch, she sipped her second cup and listened to the chatter with a smile.

Aiden had to nudge her to let her know that Eric was asking a question.

"I'm sorry?" she said, offering an apologetic smile as she set her cup on the table.

"What are you doing these days? Are you looking for a job around town?"

She scrunched her nose, barely stopping herself from saying *ew*.

"I'm good, thanks." Then, too excited to keep it to herself but not sure she was ready to share such a big step, she admitted, "I've got a lot of writing on my blog due in the next few weeks, and a few new projects I'm checking on."

"Your blog? Are you going to do something on animals again?" Cailley asked. "Those are my favorite. Much better than the ones about addicts. Those just depress me."

"But do they make you want to help?" Sage asked, arching her brows over her coffee cup.

Cailley's lips twitched, then she rolled her eyes and confessed, "Only out of guilt."

"That works." Sage laughed. Tapping into emotions was the whole point. Emotions motivated people. Maybe she'd do really well with this series of articles. She took a deep breath, wanting their opinion.

Before she could say anything, Gary pointed his cup her way. "You know, you should move away from that crazy stuff you write about and focus on the military."

Crazy stuff?

Sage bit her lip to keep from launching into a lecture on the many benefits of her making different causes public in her own small way.

It wasn't that a convivial evening with friends was the wrong place that stopped her. It was the looks on those friends' faces. Not one of them, not even AnaMaria or Cailley, seemed put out at his description. They all looked indulgently amused. Like she was a precocious kid who did parlor tricks.

For the first time ever, Sage felt self-conscious of her life choices. Did they all really think the things she cared about were crazy?

She couldn't bring herself to look at Aiden in case he wore the same expression as the rest of them.

Instead, she frowned and asked, "Why would I change my focus to the military? I know there are programs that could use more funding, like Veteran's Affairs. But they already get a lot of attention. I'm more the point-out-the-little-guy kind of blogger, you know."

"Well, sure, that's what you've done before. But now you can get serious," Eric said. "Do real work, maybe actually make a difference. You know, help Aiden out."

But she had made a difference.

Maybe she hadn't shaken the earth with her words, but she'd brought attention to shelters in need of funding or donations. She'd saved animals, helped children get schoolbooks and made connections that meant medical supplies were now readily available in a small village in Tibet.

All her blissful feelings and contentment went poof in a wave of frustration.

"Aiden doesn't need my help," she said. She forced herself to look at the man next to her. Did he think the same as everyone else? It was impossible to read him since he had that stoic military expression on his face again. "Do you?"

"I'm pretty well covered," he said quietly. "You focus on taking care of those homeless dogs and I'll take care of the military stuff."

Homeless dogs.

She stared at her coffee cup, willing the tears away. Was that all he saw she did?

Now not only was Sage's contentment gone, her stomach was churning with misery. She wanted to defend her results, but that'd feel like bragging. Like she was telling them because she needed approval. She'd never cared what others thought of her before. Was that the cost of finding bliss? Suddenly, miserably, trying to live her life for others' approval?

Maybe bliss wasn't worth it.

"We had a homeless goat through here last month," Gary told them as he refilled wine all around. "I had to chase it through the grade-school playground and the market parking lot before I cornered it."

"That's what you get for doing all your running on a treadmill," Aiden told him.

Sage gratefully let her stiff smile fade away as the discussion turned to law enforcement in Villa Rosa. She paid no attention to the talk swirling around her except to smile occasionally while lost in her own thoughts.

It didn't bother her to be considered flighty or a little eccentric. She readily acknowledged both. But that didn't mean what she did didn't deserve respect. Did Aiden feel the same way about her causes as everyone else?

An hour later, as they walked home, she was still wondering. She tucked her hand into Aiden's again and tried to set her worries aside. Since when did she care what other people thought of her? Earlier tonight, she'd figured she'd finally found bliss. Go back to that, she told her brain. Focus on the positive.

"It's a nice night for a walk, yes?"

"Sure," he agreed.

"Aren't you glad we didn't bring the car? Less pollution this way, we get a little after-dessert workout. And we have time to talk."

Like maybe about what he really thought of the things that mattered to her. The lava cake bubbled in Sage's belly like its namesake, not feeling nearly as good now as it had at dessert.

"As long as you can talk and walk at the same time," he said absently. "At least you wore flat shoes."

"And if I hadn't?"

He gave her a look. She knew he was trying for stern, but it was too amused.

"I guess I'd just have to carry you," he admitted.

"You'd do that?"

"Hey, I carried a two-hundred-pound guy with a broken leg out of the desert once. You'd be easy."

Sage's smile stiffened. Not over the reminder of what kind of things Aiden faced as a SEAL. What a contrast between what she did, what she was.

The hero and the flake.

Clearly a match made in heaven.

"You're quiet," Aiden observed.

She glanced over with a shrug.

"Just thinking."

"You usually think out loud."

"Are you trying to say I talk a lot?" she asked with a laugh.

"No. Although you do talk a lot." His grimace flashed, then was gone. "I was asking what's wrong. I figured you're upset, that's why you're so quiet."

Just like that, her lousy mood, self-doubts and pouty attitude melted away. Aiden was asking about her feelings. Since she was pretty sure he'd rather go into battle wearing a pink dress and heels while a TV crew filmed him, she knew how special that was.

Knew he'd only do it if he cared.

"What?" Aiden asked, his body suddenly as tight as his voice. "Why do you look like that?"

Sage blinked away the tears, sniffing as quietly as she could before asking, "What way? I'm fine."

"You look like you're going to cry. Stop it."

"I'm not crying," she assured him, biting her lip to keep it from wobbling.

"Sage," he warned, letting go of her hand and stepping away, as if she might explode at any second.

That, and the fierce look on his face, did it. Sage's laughter chased the tears away.

"You are so sweet," she murmured, grabbing his hand and pulling him back to her side. "I just want to cuddle you close."

"Cuddle all you want. Just don't cry." He paused, then with a sigh she felt more than heard, looked down at her. "You going to tell me what's wrong?"

He didn't really want to know. He definitely didn't want to talk feelings or deal with emotional outbursts.

But he'd do it for her.

Not because he was that kind of guy. No, Aiden didn't do things to be nice, or because it was the supposed right thing. He only did them if they had a logical sequence that he saw a need to follow.

Or because he cared.

Sage sighed, finally crossing that metaphorical line.

The one she'd been tiptoeing toward, then running from her entire life.

She'd loved Aiden forever. So you'd think the slide into being in love with him would be a simple thing. Exciting and wild, an explosion of feelings that simply took over. That's how she'd always figured love would feel.

Instead, she felt twitchy. Like her feet were itching to

run, but her body wanted to follow directions and cuddle close. Her mind raced with arguments, every one of them dismissing the idea of this being love.

But her heart just sat there, smug and sure.

She wasn't sure if this night was a dear-diary moment.

Or a good reason to take up heavy drinking.

"Sage, do me a favor."

Pulled out of her confused reverie, she glanced up at Aiden's face. Grazed by moonlight, his features were part shadow, part magic.

"Anything," she promised.

"Don't make me ask what's wrong a third time. It goes against my every instinct to try and engage a discussion on the basis of emotions."

"But you'd do it for me?"

His sigh was as light as the breeze wafting over them.

"Yeah. Somehow, with you, I find myself doing a lot of things my instincts warn against."

"For instance?"

He was silent for a second. She didn't have to glance up to know he was giving her one of those X-ray looks of his, trying to delve the secrets of her soul.

"A cozy double dinner date. A fake engagement, complete with party. A kidnapped weekend locked in a hotel room with fruit and hot fudge," he recited.

"You love fruit," she pointed out. "And while I know you're not a big sweets eater, you did lick that hot fudge clean."

"That's because it was smeared over your naked skin."

"And your instincts warn against that?"

"Too much hot fudge could lead to cavities and weight issues," he deadpanned.

Cuddling closer to his side, Sage laughed in delight.

"Ahh, look at you, taking big risks and venturing outside your comfort zone," she teased, poking him in his side.

His smirk came and went in a flash before he shook his head.

"You're not going to tell me?"

"You know, there's a reason you don't usually ask people what's on their mind that's bothering them."

"And that would be?"

"As soon as they tell you, you'd be the one bothered."

"Cute."

From his tone, he knew she was sidestepping. Sage didn't mind, though. She'd never aspired to be the mysterious type. Until tonight, she'd never aspired to be any type other than who she was. Mostly because she'd never thought twice about how other people might view her.

Until tonight.

"Can I ask you something?" she said hesitantly.

"You just did," he pointed out, smiling down at her.

Right. Why was it easier to get naked and eat chocolate off of a guy than ask a simple question?

"You can ask another one," he prompted. "I'll tell you anything unless it's top secret, classified or none of your civilian business."

"Lucky for you I have no interest in military secrets. This is about me," she told him.

"You want to tell me your secrets?" He sounded hesitant. Like he wanted to know, but didn't want to want to know.

"Maybe." She bit her lip, then forced herself to quit being coy and just spit it out. "Do you think what I do is a waste of time?"

"What you do? You mean, your various jobs?" Before she could correct him, and yes, she did hesitate because she was suddenly just as interested in his response to that as she was her actual question, he continued. "No. I think you're looking for your right fit. While you look, you're adding a variety of skills to your résumé and staying busy."

He made it sound so clever, noble even. Sage would have done a happy dance right then and there, except it would mean letting go of Aiden. And as good as she was feeling right now, she had a lot of plans for his body that required holding on tight.

"You don't think I'm a flake?"

"I think the term that fits you best is free spirit."

"I like that image," she decided. "It makes me sound like I should be running around outdoors, naked."

"I like *that* image," he decided with the husky laugh she'd happily come to recognize as his horny alert.

Mmm, decisions, decisions.

The temptation to go the naked route was overwhelming.

But she'd come this far. And while she might be a free spirit, she wasn't a chicken. So she resisted the urge to pull her dress over her head.

"Actually, I meant my blog. You know, the posts I write. The causes I try to bring attention to. Do you think it's a waste of time?"

"You've found homes for how many dogs?" he asked, tugging her off the path and over to the little gazebo at the base of the hill.

"Thirty or so," she said. She pulled her hand free so she had both free to wave over her head. As if it were a vague number that didn't matter instead of thirty-two beautiful, loyal animals who now had safe, loving homes.

"How much did you raise for that water project in Africa last year?"

"You knew about that?" She wished the moon was brighter so she could see his face. Instead, it was shrouded in shadows, so all she could go on were his words. And those were surprising the hell out of her.

"You blogged about it, didn't you?"

"You really do read my blog?" Now she was grateful for the lack of light, since there was nothing attractive about her jaw hanging open.

"Of course I read it. I've donated, too. Not always, but whenever I can. I've been known to nag guys to donate sometimes, as well," he admitted, laughing quietly as he held out his hand to lead her up the steps of the gazebo.

"You got your big bad navy pals to donate to my causes?" she asked, delighted.

"Hey, some guys push their daughters' or nieces' Girl Scout cookies. I push charitable causes." His shrug was uncomfortable, like he wanted to brush off the conversation as fast as possible. "Look, it's no big deal."

"It is to me," she admitted, lifting first one of his hands, then the other, to her mouth and brushing a kiss over his knuckles. "It means everything to me."

"You're kidding, right?"

Sage blinked hard, not sure where the tears had come from or why, but knowing they were the bittersweet happy kind that she couldn't run from.

After all, they were falling-in-love tears.

She'd have to be crazy to run from falling in love. Wouldn't she?

"Of course I'm not kidding," she told him, trying to stay focused on the conversation and not her freaked-out thoughts. "Other than my father, who I secretly suspect believes in me more for the sake of faith in genetics than his being impressed with my choices, you're the only person to ever show faith in me."

"Your friends have faith in you."

Right. She almost laughed, then realized he actually meant that. Her brow creased as she mulled that over.

Did they?

"Well, I suppose they have faith that I'll entertain them," she said after a moment. "They figure my next blog post will make them laugh, or give them something to wonder about over lunch."

"But that's the charm of your writing," he pointed out. "Your articles are so entertaining, they make people want to donate to be a part of the fun."

"I like how you put that," she decided, wrapping her arms around his waist. "It sounds much better than my friends all think I'm a flake."

"THAT'S STUPID," Aiden growled. It'd been bad enough earlier, listening to Eric make light of Sage's blog and the causes she supported. But hearing her do it was just too much.

She was an incredible woman and in all the years he'd known her, she'd always seemed very aware of that.

This new self-doubt thing was pure crap. She had to stop and get back to appreciating her unique awesomeness.

"Oh, I'm not saying they don't care about me. They're wonderful friends and great people. But I'm not really like them. And they don't expect me to be," she said with a light laugh. If it wasn't for the uncertainty he'd heard in her voice, he'd think she was totally cool with the dismissal of her projects.

If she wanted to pretend, he should let her. These emotional discussions, pushing her to open up and confess emotions, it was crazy.

"You've never cared before what people thought," he said, unable to let it go. "What changed?"

Her sigh was deep enough to ruffle the leaves on the far-off trees.

"I guess it's because I don't feel solid in where I'm at, you know? Usually, I'm focused, on a quest of one sort or other. Then it doesn't bother me that I'm a novelty to most people. A source of curiosity."

"But now?"

"But now, I'm not sure what I want to do. For the first time, I have no quest. No purpose. Maybe it's just my dad's situation that has me questioning things, you know." Her voice dropped, then she lifted her chin and gave him a wobbly smile. "What you do, it makes a huge difference in the world. It probably saves the world."

When Aiden cringed she gave a light laugh before adding, "Gary makes a difference to the town. My dad makes a difference in students' lives."

"So?" Those were just their jobs.

"So? I've never lasted at anything long enough to make seniority, let alone make a difference."

Aiden shook his head, baffled that a woman as assured and confident as Sage could think something like that.

"I'd ask if you were kidding, but I can see you aren't," he said, brushing his finger over her damp cheek. "I wish I were a poet, or gifted with words. Then I could explain how important I think what you do is. You bring passion and energy to these things, Sage. Whether they are big things that shake the world or not is immaterial. They matter to you. And they matter to others."

"You really think that?" she asked, her words husky. But her smile was there, just at the edges of her mouth.

Feeling like he'd just escaped falling off a cliff, the tension started seeping out of Aiden's shoulders as he smiled back at her.

"Of course I think that. I wouldn't have said it otherwise. You know that."

There. That should comfort her just fine.

Aiden barely resisted a smug pat on her shoulder.

A good thing, since two seconds later she burst into tears.

Crap.

Crap, crap, crap.

Rarely felt panic gripping him, Aiden looked around, desperate for a solution. An answer. Hell, an escape.

Nothing.

"Sage," he said. But he had nothing to follow it up with. He lifted his hands, wanting to hold her but afraid she'd cry more.

At his move, she gave a deep, shuddering sob, then lifted her chin. She wet her lips, her eyes locking on his.

"Are you okay?" he asked hesitantly.

"I'm more than okay. I'm wonderful," she assured him. As she did, her fingers worked some kind of magic at her waist, sending her skirt floating like a purple cloud to her feet.

"What're you doing?" he asked. Not that he was going to stop her, whatever it was. Anything that involved Sage and naked skin was okay in his book.

"I promised you naughty sexual favors on the walk home, remember?" She let her blouse drop to the gazebo floor, where it pooled on top of her skirt.

Aiden looked around.

They were on her dad's property, but it wasn't exactly private. He didn't see signs of anyone around, though. And, he realized as his gaze shifted back where it belonged— on Sage's silken skin—he didn't care.

This was a mistake. Continuing this affair was only going to make ending it harder.

But, ending it was already going to be hard enough. He was sentencing himself to a life without Sage when this was over. So shouldn't he have a few more memories to get him through that long, lonely future?

That was all sad, sad justification.

Again, he didn't care.

He wanted her.

Here, now.

Naked.

Slow, intense and hot.

With that in mind, he silently followed her lead, letting his clothes fall to the floor with hers.

They didn't say another word.

In silence, just the sound of their breath and the wind lightly rustling through the trees, they worshipped each other's bodies.

Lips slid together, fingers skimmed.

Her nipples pebbled against his palms, beckoning to his mouth. Her body melted against his like a gossamer wish, delicate and sweet and everything he'd ever been afraid to dream of in a life filled with violence.

As he slid into her welcoming warmth, their breath mingled. Their hearts beat in sync.

And Aiden was deathly afraid he'd just stepped over into an emotional minefield that there was no escape from.

But as he watched Sage's moonlit-dappled face fade into passion, he realized he simply didn't care.

With her, the emotions, and their cost, were worth it.

11

So THIS WAS WHAT normal life felt like.

A ten-mile run at daybreak, then breakfast with a buddy at Tilly's. A visit with the dean at the university to chat about options that Aiden had no intention of taking but was flattered to hear. Now an after-lunch chess game with his mentor.

Aiden wasn't sure he'd ever felt so content.

Then again, he couldn't remember ever before having fallen asleep in the arms of a woman like Sage or waking up to a body so incredible, eight mornings in a row.

The run, breakfast, the job offer and even the game were great.

But Sage...

Aiden gave a satisfied smile.

Sage was incredible.

"You seem peaceful. That's something I've rarely seen."

Seated across from the Professor, Aiden contemplated the older man's insight and the chessboard at the same time.

"It's been a good trip." Wincing, Aiden lifted his gaze and pulled a face. "I don't mean your illness, of course."

Lee laughed, the sound almost as hearty as it used to

be. That, and the pink of his skin, reassured Aiden that he wasn't making a mistake heading back to Coronado in a few days.

"Life doesn't stop because one man becomes ill, Aiden. Nor should your pleasure in that life." The older man smiled, looking as pleased as if he'd just won the game, found out his fall classes were wait-listed and got his hands on another vintage encyclopedia set to add to his collection. "You're in a great place in your life. Young, healthy and in love with, if you'll forgive the bias, a wonderful woman."

Aiden's smile didn't shift. He didn't acknowledge the tension that gripped his gut, nor did he even blink at the pain that pulsed in his temple. No point.

The other man was right.

About all of it.

Since Aiden wasn't willing to discuss his feelings for Sage—even with himself—he simply smiled and moved his knight.

"You return to duty soon?" the Professor asked quietly, contemplating his next move.

"I'm due on base Monday," Aiden confirmed quietly, not sure how he felt about that. Brow creased, he looked across the table at the Professor, trying to gauge how he was really doing. He looked good. He and Dr. Brooke felt his response to the experimental treatments was even better than they'd hoped.

Aiden wasn't naive. He'd lost people in his life. Important people. So his goodbyes in the past had always included the simple knowledge that he might not see the other man again. More because of the very real hazards of his duty than because he thought the old guy was going to keel over while he was away.

But this time it was different.

"Are you comfortable with me leaving?" he asked quietly.

"Are you comfortable leaving?" the Professor shot back in his typical way. At Aiden's arch look, he laughed and shrugged. "There's no reason for you to ignore your duty. I'm in good shape and out of danger for now. There is a very real chance of remission. I've even told the dean that I'll return to teaching this fall. So yes, I'm comfortable."

Aiden nodded.

"Besides, Sage is here."

Aiden's nod turned into a jerk of his chin. He tried to disguise it by clearing his throat and gave the old guy a searching look.

"You don't believe she'll stick around?" the Professor asked with a knowing smile. "Here, in Villa Rosa, I mean."

"Once you've recovered?" Aiden asked. Then he winced, vowing to pay as much attention to his words as he did the game from now on.

"Good point. And an interesting one coming from her fiancé."

Maybe a little *more* attention to his words. He could win the game later.

"Isn't knowing each other well an important requirement for an engaged couple?" he asked.

"I don't think it's ever possible to know everything about each other," the Professor mused. "And as much as you think you know now, you'll find there's so much more to learn after the wedding."

"That's a part of the adventure, I'd imagine."

"Indeed it is." After a long pause, the older man moved his pawn. "But you don't think Sage will stay in Villa Rosa after the doctor declares me in remission?"

"If you wanted her to, she would try," Aiden said, opting for the safest response.

"But?"

"Sage isn't a homebody. She loves seeing new things,

exploring the world and meeting people," Aiden pointed out. "Just because she's engaged doesn't mean she's got anchors on her wings."

"Marriage might make her reconsider."

"I don't think that's a good argument for getting married then," Aiden replied, laughing. "Since graduating high school, the longest she's lived in one place is eight months. I don't see that changing."

"That's been well and good so far, but it needs to change. She hasn't been happy the last couple of years. Until now, until the two of you became engaged." Misinterpreting Aiden's look, the other man waved one hand. "No, no, don't get me wrong. I'm not putting the burden of my daughter's happiness on your shoulders. I'm just saying that with you, she seems to have finally found that something she's always been looking for."

Or she was faking it really well for her father's peace of mind.

"Sage missed out on a lot, growing up without a mother. Because I was so involved in my studies, my work, I think she never quite felt grounded. To use one of her new-age terms," the Professor added with a smile.

Aiden figured it was a credit to the guy's fathering that he knew the terms, that he cared so much about his daughter that he'd bothered to learn her lingo, her interests. Since the older man didn't seem to be waiting for a response, Aiden kept his observation quiet, though.

"She's found that touchstone with you, I think. Which would make it much easier for her to find peace as well."

"Do you think she's really looking for peace?" Aiden asked, not wanting to argue but figuring that was the sort of thing Sage was saving for old age.

"I think she could be happy finding it. Happier still

if she were settled. A home, a family. A husband who is around to enjoy those things with her."

Fury hit him like a freight train named jealousy.

"You think she should marry someone else?"

"Oh, no," the other man protested, leaning forward to give Aiden's knee a reassuring pat. "Of course not. The two of you, you're perfect for each other."

Trying to tamp down the anger, Aiden frowned. What was the old man getting at then?

"But I think that marriage has challenges, any marriage. And those challenges are best dealt with if both parties are together, in one place."

Aha. Finally caught up, Aiden puffed out a breath.

"Sage isn't the type to live in base housing. All the buildings looking alike would drive her crazy before she even unpacked. But don't worry, we'll figure it out," he said, making the fake promise sound as sincere as he could.

After all, if they really were engaged, they could easily work that out. Coronado had a lot to offer, but if Sage didn't want to live there, San Diego was close enough. She loved warm weather and beaches, it was right up her alley.

"I was thinking more along the lines of the two of you settling here, in Villa Rosa."

"I'm stationed in Southern California."

Talk about stating the obvious.

But Aiden was pretty sure he wasn't going to like where this conversation was going, so he figured obvious was the safest option available.

"You know, the dean would be happy to have you teach classes while you finish your degrees, get your master's. You're a few classes away from, what? Three separate degrees?"

"Four," Aiden corrected with a shrug. Some people figured it was his time commitment with the navy that prevented him from finishing those degrees. But the reality was, a degree would mean choices.

Choices it looked like he might have to soon justify not making.

"That's a nice offer, and I appreciate it. But I've got a career and I'm not looking for a change." He absently moved his rook, then shrugged. "Not in careers, not even in bumping up from enlisted to officer, which that first degree would get me."

"Don't you think it's telling that you've avoided taking that step all these years?"

More telling that somewhere in the back of his mind he'd always known that a degree would come along with this exact conversation. And, again, those damned choices.

"You've what? Another year in the service?"

"I'd planned on another twenty, to tell you the truth."

"But you could get out in a year if you had a promising career that would make your new wife happy, don't you think?"

Aiden stared at the older man over his steepled fingers. For the last dozen years, his mentor had stood in silent support of Aiden's military career. Now, all of a sudden, the guy was encouraging him to get out? Because Aiden was engaged to his daughter? Or, just as likely knowing Professor Taylor, because he sensed Aiden's discontent and figured it was time to ask those difficult questions that made his protégé have to think.

"And maybe I spend those next couple of years finishing up those degrees, get my master's, so I could hit the university with a solid start?" Aiden guessed. Correctly, he saw when the other man nodded. "And while I do all of this, what will Sage be doing?"

He couldn't imagine her doing anything that made her

happy here, in Villa Rosa. At least, not for more than a few months.

Then again, was there anywhere that would make her happy for more than a few months? Despite his earlier words, he was sure Coronado wouldn't do it. He didn't think the entire state of California, with all of its vast appeal, could keep her entertained for more than a year.

And while he had no doubt he could keep her happy, keep her entertained, he wasn't around all the time. Hell, he wasn't around most of the time.

Aiden glared at the chessboard, wondering if the old man was right. If this engagement between Sage and himself was real, the only way it'd work between them was if he left the military. If he was around, 24/7, to devote himself to keeping her happy.

It was a little terrifying just how appealing that image was. How easily he could see himself leaving the SEALs, giving up his current way of life and settling down here to work his way into being a stodgy old professor.

Then again, how long would Sage be content with a stodgy old professor?

"The two of you will have a wonderful future," Lee said quietly. "You just have to decide what you want that future to be, then make it happen."

Right. Because he had not one single viable option to choose from. But he just had to pick and make it happen.

"Just think about it," the older man requested with an avuncular smile. Right before he checked Aiden's queen.

Staring at the board, wondering when he'd lost control, Aiden could only grit his teeth.

It wasn't that the Professor would ask that bothered Aiden. The guy was just looking out for what he thought was best for his daughter.

It was that the request held so much appeal.

And was as stupid as jumping out of a plane without a chute.

That's what made Aiden want to put his fist through a wall.

FILLED WITH NERVES, Sage paced the doorstep in front of Aiden's cottage a few times, trying to get a grip on herself. She had so much to tell him. It'd be a lot easier if she knew if she was happy, excited or just freaked before she did.

She'd made a commitment.

A big one.

Instead of trying the writing job on for size, a few articles here and there, she'd not only committed to a permanent position but had agreed to scary things. Like insurance and a 401k.

And now she was hoping to make yet another one. This one with '*til death do we part* potential.

She had to force herself not to wring her hands and whimper. Instead, she sucked in a deep breath and gave a quick rat-a-tat-tat on Aiden's front door.

"Knock, knock," she echoed, opening the door and sticking her head inside.

Oh, my.

Aiden looked as if his day was in an ugly downward spiral, and hadn't come close to finishing its descent.

Maybe she should leave.

Ensconced on the sofa, he was looking at something. And it wasn't making him happy.

He gave her a look she couldn't read. Which made it really hard to know if it'd be better to go in and seduce him into a smile or ask if she could borrow an egg and run.

"C'mon in," he told her in a chilly tone.

Did she have to? Biting her lip, Sage lifted the basket

she'd left on the porch, plastered a cheery smile on her face and went over seduction scenarios in her head.

"What're you doing?" she asked, setting a basket on the coffee table before joining him on the couch. She tilted her head to look at what was in his lap. "Ooh, I haven't seen that in a long time."

Setting aside her worry over his mood, she melted at the images in his lap. He was so cute. She tapped her finger on the photo album, leaning close enough that her hair slid over his arm.

"You look so much like your mom," she noted. "I don't think I realized that. Of course, I don't remember her well. Mostly the cookies she brought me to snack on while you were being tutored by my dad."

"It was a long time ago," Aiden said, closing the album and tossing it next to her basket.

"You must miss them a lot." Her words were quiet, sympathetic. Since he didn't look like he'd welcome it, she didn't move. But she wanted so badly to reach out and wrap him in a tight hug.

"Yeah, well it's been a long time." As if sensing her hugging urges, he pushed away from the couch and strode over to the window to stare out. "I've got plenty to keep me busy, you know."

What was up? She couldn't figure out if he was sad, angry or what. He was definitely not himself, though. Trying to figure out the best tack to take to get him back to happy, Sage leaned forward, opening the basket she'd brought and digging inside.

"Are you thirsty?" she asked, pretending she wasn't gauging every second of his mood. "I brought champagne. I have chocolate cake in here, too. Cheese and crackers, some grapes and strawberries, two containers of Mrs. Green's macaroni salad, and more chocolate."

That got his attention.

Aiden turned from contemplating the window to give her a baffled expression.

"Why?"

"Well, you can never have too much chocolate," she said with a straight face.

"And the rest of the picnic?"

"I was hungry. And I wanted to celebrate."

The feast spread over the table now, she held out a small plate. He eyed her stubbornly cheerful expression for a moment, then sighed and walked over. He didn't take the plate, though. Just stared at the food.

"Aren't you hungry?" she asked, hoping he'd correctly interpret that to mean *what's the matter and how can I make it better?*

"I had lunch a couple of hours ago."

So much for his interpretive skills. Sage bit her lip, giving the champagne more attention than it needed. This wasn't quite going as easily as she'd hoped.

"What are you celebrating?"

Her. Not them.

What the heck was grumping him out? Sage clenched her teeth into a stiff smile and fished the flutes out of the basket. Clearly she was going to have to dig past his mood before they could get to the fun stuff.

"No thanks," he said when she started to pour the second glass.

"You'd make me celebrate alone?" A chill danced down her spine. She was starting to get the feeling that she'd be doing a lot more than celebrating alone. "Would you rather have a soda? Scotch? A shot of tequila?"

"You have all of that in your basket there?"

"You'd be amazed at what I have in my basket here,"

she teased. Then, hoping he'd change his mind, she poured the second glass and silently set it on the table.

"So?" he prompted impatiently. "You still haven't said what you're celebrating."

She'd hoped to be celebrating a little togetherness. Possibly share a few whispered maybes and tentative possibilities?

Maybe after she shared her news and they sipped a little bubbly he'd share his grump and she could fix it. The only way she'd find out if it'd work was to get started.

"I've got a new job… No," she corrected, taking a deep breath to try and calm the nerves bouncing in her belly. She lifted her glass. "A career."

His eyes lit for a brief second, then the delight washed away, leaving that military stoicism she loved so much.

"You? A career?" He shook his head. "Next you're going to tell me you want to go to work on Wall Street peddling fake stocks to bilk little old ladies out of their life savings."

"Eww, yuck. But you're right, that's pretty close to my definition of a career. At least, it was before."

Before she'd lost that always nagging urge to run that'd dogged her for so many years. Contentment wrapped around her, as comfortable as a warm, cozy blanket.

"I took a position with this great publisher who's been trying to get me to write for them for years. Usually, I just send them an article or two when I needed money, but I figured with everything going on," she waved her hand to indicated that vague everything, "I'd like something a little more settled."

"You mean you're going to write a few articles for them?"

"No, I've actually agreed to be a monthly columnist for two of their publications, as well as write a series of articles. One about the climate, another on aging pets."

"You signed a contract?"

She wrinkled her nose at the shock in his tone.

"Sure," she said. Suddenly starving, she grabbed a handful of grapes from the table, popping a couple in her mouth. "I figured my dad has that surgery next week, so I'll be here for at least the next month or two. That gives me time to get used to it, and it'll keep my mind off things after you're gone."

"You're serious?"

"I am. I'm really excited about it, too," she told him, feeling that same content joy she had earlier when she'd got off the phone with the editor. "I think I've finally found my perfect focus, you know?"

"You think so?"

Brows creased at his tone, she inspected his face trying to see what was going on in there.

"I do think so," she said, still looking. "It's a mobile sort of job so I can do it from here while my dad's still recovering, then from, you know, wherever I want later."

Like, maybe down south on the naval base. Or in Coronado, in a cute little beachside place off base with a view and room for a garden.

"Handy benefit," Aiden said quietly, his look still so distant she felt like he was already back in Coronado.

"I want to do a few articles, write my column for a month or so to get settled into the idea of a deadline. Then, in a month or so after my dad is stable, I was thinking it'd be cool to come to the navy base. I'd like to check out the military angle. You know, there are a lot of great programs out there, but some that don't get any attention. I could help with that."

"What? Military angles? Why?"

"Because they are important," she said quietly. "I figured I'd do my usual thing. Talk to people, hang out, get an idea for what feels right. I was hoping I could run my list by you once I get rolling?" she said with a wide grin. She all but clapped her hands together, she was so excited. "Just to see what you think of them from an official military angle."

"What brought all of this on?"

"It's been in my head ever since dinner the other night," she admitted, pacing in front of the couch as all the possibilities danced through her head. "Eric's suggestion that I write something that's more military seemed silly at first, but the more I thought about it, the more ideas I've had."

"Don't."

"What?"

"Don't change your life around. Especially not right now. Things are in flux, emotionally off-kilter because of everything that's been going on."

Sage stopped pacing. Not because she didn't want to keep moving, but because her stomach was starting to churn and she figured staying still was smarter.

"Which everything might you be referring to?" she asked in her best professor's daughter tone.

"Your father's health, for one."

"He's doing a lot better. He's stable enough for pancreatic surgery, and his odds of recovery from that are good." That didn't mean she wasn't worried. But Dr. Brooke had assured her that this was a long road. It'd be silly to put her life on hold until they reached a new fork.

"Look, Sage, this is crazy." He pushed his hand through his short hair and gave her a look of pure frustration. "You're buying into this facade, the whole settling down, engaged couple, Villa Rosa future."

She bit her lip. Facade?

Sure, their engagement was fake. But that didn't mean their feelings were. At least, hers weren't.

"I'm pretty clear on what's fake and what's real," she pointed out gently. Getting angry was pointless. Besides, it'd ruin the celebration before they got to the naked parts.

"Sure, okay," he agreed in a tone that said the exact opposite. She'd never wanted to take a pillow and smack him upside the head more than she did in that moment.

"I know real from fake, Aiden. Our engagement is fake. My loving you is real," she blurted out.

Oh, hell. Panic surged through her system like a tornado, wreaking emotional destruction. Sage pressed her fingers against her lips in horror. Had she actually said that aloud?

Maybe it was frustration. It could have been the sight of his untouched champagne next to the photos of him as a little boy with his mother. Or maybe she'd simply kept it to herself for way too long.

It didn't matter what it was. If his expression was anything to go by, she'd have been better to stuff her face *into* a pillow.

"You know, that's the kind of admission a girl usually hopes will garner a happy reaction. Maybe a hug, a reciprocal declaration." She folded her arms over her chest, as if that flimsy move would protect her heart. "But, hey, your look of *oh, shit* is appealing, too."

"You don't love me," he told her, shaking his head. He sounded so sure, she almost nodded in automatic agreement.

Catching herself, she frowned instead.

"I think I know what I'm feeling," she said tightly. At least, she was pretty sure she did.

"Sure, you think you do. But this is what you do, Sage. You throw yourself into the situation wholeheartedly. You've been playing loving fiancée so well, you've actually convinced yourself you love me." He grimaced, then added in a tone that made her want to kick him, "Next thing, you'll be convincing yourself that this engagement should be real instead of pretend."

She clenched her teeth against the pain of hearing him dismiss her feelings, and her secret hope, so blithely. It wasn't as though she really believed they had a chance. Or that she thought either of them, she or he, were marriage material.

But, dammit, she knew what she was feeling.

Before she could tell him that, he frowned, then sighed.

"Look, Sage, how many guys have you tried to save in your life? You get into their world, become their counselor, their nursemaid, their cheering section." He waved all that away as if he were in need of, oh, absolutely nothing she had to offer. Then, as if afraid she hadn't gotten the message, he added a verbal confirmation. "I don't need that."

"Are you saying you don't care about me?"

He might not need what she had to offer. But the only way she'd be able to get past her own need to give him something, anything, besides her heart, was to hear it from his own mouth.

Aiden stared at his hands as if he were trying to gather his thoughts together. Finally, he met her gaze again.

"I do love you," he admitted quietly. She took a quick breath, ready to explode with delight. Before she could say anything, before she even knew what to say, he shook his head. "But that's not enough."

"I love you and you love me. And that's not enough?" she said faintly, her hands twisting together to keep from tossing them in the air at the craziness of that statement. "I'm sorry, Aiden. But I think that's more than enough."

"Look, the odds against marital success in the military are long. They're even steeper in the SEALs. My team has had three guys pair up in the last few years. I figure they've called dibs on the positive relationship accomplishments for our platoon."

"You don't really believe that we don't have a chance because someone else claimed the good relationship mojo first, do you?" Her words were somewhere between amused and baffled.

"I'm saying we don't have a chance," he clarified.

"Why?"

Aiden looked as if he was steeling himself for battle. His shoulders were stiff and his chin high. The expression on his face, so distant and dismissive, made her stomach churn.

"You're not the kind to stick around, Sage. You flit from one quest to another. From this relationship to that, job after city after guy."

"You're saying I'm a flake?"

"Are you saying you aren't?"

He thought she was too flaky to be in love with him? Or that she was too flaky to love? Since both options sucked, she didn't bother to ask. Instead, her chin high, Sage took a deep breath. This conversation was humiliating enough. She'd be damned if she'd top it off by crying.

"What brought this on?" she finally asked.

"You, this crazy declaration. Your father and his grand plans for our life." He waved his hand in the general direction of her father's house, where she supposed the Professor had detailed the same grand plans for Aiden as he had for her.

"That's it? You're declaring us impossible because my father has some silly idea of how we should live our lives?"

"No. I'm simply declaring us impossible."

Oh. Sage swallowed hard to get past the knotted misery in her throat. Well, then.

"You know what? I've got this reputation for running

through life, unable to commit to anything." Fueled by fury-inspired insights, she jabbed an accusatory finger at him. "But you're the one who's actually running."

"Sage..."

"No," she interrupted before he could finish whatever he planned to say in that placating, condescending tone. "Here's the difference between us, Aiden. I might be running, but I'm running toward things. I'm chasing my dreams. But you? You're running from life."

"Me? Running from life? That's such a bunch of crap." He leaned in so close his breath ruffled the hair all the way on the *back* of her head. "I'm a SEAL, Sage. I don't run from anything."

"You're running from your past. You're running from decisions. You're running from dealing with my emotions and the possibilities the two of us offer each other."

"You're talking crazy," he said, dismissively.

That was it. Sage's emotions exploded like a potato in a microwave, splattering all over the place in ugly chunks.

"At least I'm willing to try. At least I'm not a coward," she said, her jaw clenched so tight her throat hurt.

Not as much as his probably did, the way his mouth dropped open.

"You're calling me a coward?"

"I am." Letting the rare anger wash over her, wrapping herself in the comfort of it, she offered a glare. "Physically, you are the bravest man I know. You risk everything for your country."

His icy stare thawed a smidge.

"But emotionally, you're still seventeen. You won't take any emotional risks, you won't let anyone get close to you."

"Bullshit."

"Name one."

"Your father," he said, his words snapped tight.

"First off, your relationship with my father is as close to purely intellectual as it's possible to get. The two of you are two volumes of the same encyclopedia."

"Nice."

"And secondly," she continued, talking right over his sarcasm, "you've already emotionally disconnected. You saw this entire engagement as a way to pay him back. To pay your dues. As far as you're concerned, we might as well hold the funeral."

"That's crap," he snapped, the ice gone now as hot fury took over his expression. "I'll be damned if you'll dismiss my relationship with the Professor so blithely."

"Are you saying you didn't go along with our charade of an engagement because you felt as if you owed him?"

"Of course I owe him. And I care about him and respect him." Aiden gave her a look that said she was going to have to do a lot better than that. "Do you have a point?"

"Of course I do." She had to take a deep breath, steeling herself against it, though. "Do you think my father will recover from this cancer? That he'll live to see Christmas?"

His silence broke her heart.

"You go on back to hiding in the navy, Aiden," she suggested, her voice thick with tears. "I'll stay here and deal with real life."

"What are you going to do?" he asked.

She had to give him credit for not rising to the bait. But that was Aiden. He only dealt in logic, never in emotions.

Wanting it all to be over so badly she could taste it, Sage got to her feet and slowly made her way to the door. Her body ached, as if it'd taken a beating right along with her heart.

Hand on the knob, she turned back to face Aiden. He had that stoic, emotionless look on his face. The one that made her want to either hug him tight or hit him in the head with a pillow.

"We had an agreement," she said quietly. "The rules of our engagement, remember? And even though you think I'm a complete flake, I don't back out of my agreements."

With that, and one last look at him and that damned stoic expression of his, Sage walked out. She made it all the way to the bottom of the hill before she lost it.

Tears streaming down her cheeks, Sage wrapped her arms around herself and stared at her father's house in the distance.

Instead of celebrating, she'd blown their entire relationship all to hell.

12

"ARE YOU FREAKING kidding me?" Aiden glared at the lousy cards in his hand, then threw them on the table so hard they scattered cash into the lap of the guy across from him.

"Dude, you are one grumpy mother." Castillo grinned as he plucked a five and twelve ones off of himself.

Aiden clenched his teeth to keep the threat of an official reprimand from flying out.

Not because he had a problem smacking down insubordination, even if it was from a friend. Nope. What kept his mouth shut was that, officially, Castillo outranked him.

Aiden dropped his head and sighed.

And, yeah, that Castillo was a friend.

"What's your problem?" the friend asked, pushing back from the table and making a show of counting his money as he crossed the room.

"I've got a lot on my mind," Aiden muttered, scooping up the cards to deal a round of solitaire. A game he should be good at, considering he'd be going it alone. "I just need time to sort it out."

"You've had time. And distractions. Whatever's in there ain't gonna sort itself. So maybe you should tell ole Castillo your woes and there ya go, quick as a snap—" which he demonstrated by snapping his fingers, the sound echoing like a shotgun blast through the barracks "—I'll fix up your life."

Aiden smirked. At six-four, two-twenty pounds of muscle, and Auntie as his call sign, Castillo was known for being bossy, pushy and, damn the man, always right. His cocky attitude, quick fist and ready hand to a friend made Aiden grateful he was on their side. But his insistence on fixing everything, everyone, was irritating at best. Hence, his call sign.

"I don't need fixing," Aiden said.

"You're gonna keep throwing the cards around, copping an attitude and being a pain in my ass, you do."

Three weeks back from leave, two days back from a training session in the Atlantic and Aiden was still in the same lousy funk he'd been in when he'd flown out of San Francisco.

He'd figured it'd take a couple days, max, to get over missing Sage. That's all it'd ever taken before.

Of course, they'd never had sex before. They'd never been engaged before, nor had he been a complete dick and broken her heart before.

He figured all that would take at least an extra couple of weeks to get over.

He stared at the cards laid out on the table, not seeing a single move. Maybe because he'd made the wrong choice? He looked around the stark barracks, his bunk and wall-locker as barren and boring as the rest of the room. Was giving up all that, hurting Sage, worth this?

"You ever had to make a choice? A tough one?" Aiden asked quietly. Not looking up, he pulled the cards back into a stack and reshuffled.

"Life or death?"

Aiden grimaced, not surprised at Castillo's tone. Yeah,

yeah. Given the type of missions they went on, the objectives they carried out, that was a stupid question.

Crap. This talking about stuff was hard.

He debated sidestepping.

But, dammit, three weeks and he was still in a funk.

Clearly he wasn't getting himself out on his own.

"No. More like, directions," he decided with a vague wave of his hand. "Life."

"I had to choose between a curvy blonde and a lithe redhead once," Castillo said, dropping to his bunk, folding his hands behind his head and grinning. "Tough decision, given that they were both naked and offering up all sorts of enticements."

"That's not quite the life decision I was talking about." Halfway through dealing out his solitaire pyramid, Aiden shot an arch look across the room.

"It was a life changer, my friend."

"I'm sure." Aiden dealt a hand of solitaire, his eyes locked on the cards.

"Don't you want to know what I did?"

"I can live without the details."

"Suit yourself." With a wide grin, Castillo reached under his bunk and grabbed a small knapsack and started pulling out supplies.

"What the hell are you doing?" Aiden asked, eyeing the sports sock, blue buttons and a surgery-sized needle dangling thread.

"My nana sent me instructions for making a poppet. Sorta like a voodoo doll, but not."

Despite his lousy mood, Aiden laughed.

"You're making a Banks doll?"

The big guy glanced up from his awkward attempt to sew the toe into the shape of a head. His blue eyes were about as innocent as a three-year-old's, and his expression pure as an altar boy. Yeah. He was up to something.

"A Banks doll? That'd be against protocol. I'm just researching a little family tradition. Sorta like an experiment."

"That Banks's sock?" Aiden asked, having read enough about indigenous beliefs to have a pretty good idea what the experiment involved. Since he had no belief himself in the possibility of it working, he didn't bother asking about the hoped-for outcome.

If Castillo's sewing was anything to go by, though, Banks's head was in danger of falling off. Before or after he got a major belly ache and went bald.

"Found the sock in the laundry," Castillo muttered, wincing when he stabbed the needle into his thumb. He wiped the blood on the cuff of the sock. Whether it was part of the ritual, or just sloppy sewing, he made a show of rubbing it in real good.

"Banks's sock?" Aiden asked.

"Could be." Castillo squinted over his sock project. "Got a problem with that?"

"As long as you stay outta my socks, I don't care what you do," Aiden decided. The last guy who'd had a problem with Castillo was an air-force jet jockey, and he'd ended up in the infirmary.

"Why do you have such a beef with the guy?" Aiden asked. "We've teamed with plenty of gung-ho, by-the-book, medal junkies. You've always taken it in stride before."

"Dunno." Castillo shrugged. "Why don't we talk about those life choices that've got you all pissy. Then we can talk beef."

Right.

Aiden tilted his head, conceding the point.

Before he could figure out if he wanted any more of
Castillo's questionable advice—because hello, who needed
to think when the choice was between a blonde and a
redhead?—the barracks door opened.

Petty Officer Brody Lane strode in.

"Yo, Castillo. Masters," he said in greeting as he crossed
the room.

Aiden responded with an absent nod, more interested in
how Brody was moving than whatever he had to say. Even
after two weeks of maneuvers, the guy moved with ease.
Good. That meant he was completely recovered from the
injury that'd jacked up his leg and almost taken him out
of the game earlier that year.

"You've got company," Brody said, tossing his cap on
his bed before snagging his stack of mail off the table.
The guy lived two hours away from his fiancée, saw her
often enough that his toothbrush barely had time to dry,
and she'd still sent him at least a half-dozen letters. Hell,
she'd have had to be writing some of those when he was
lying in bed next to her.

Love. It was crazy.

"What company?" Aiden asked.

"Pretty lady. Didn't want to talk to you here in the barracks," Brody said, one eye on Aiden while thumbing
through his mail. "She's in the Joint Reception Center."

She?

Why she would visit him on base?

Dammit. Aiden sighed. As if he needed to wonder.

"Sage is here?" he asked, tossing his cards on the table,
not caring that they sent the others flying. Clearly, he was
through playing solitaire.

"Sage Taylor," Brody acknowledged with a nod. His
tone was casual, but the look in his eyes was piercing.
"She claims she's your fiancée."

Aiden didn't have to glance over to see that Castillo was looking just as intrigued.

Shit.

"You're engaged?"

No. Before he could deny it, rule three flashed through his brain. Dammit.

"Yeah. Sorta." He shrugged. "We had a fight."

"Ahhh, one that made you question life directions," Castillo surmised with a grin, pointing the sock at Aiden.

"I don't want to talk about it," Aiden said, not willing to have this discussion. Now, or ever. He grabbed his cap out of his back pocket and pulled it down to shade his eyes. "Can't keep my fiancée waiting while I hang around chit-chatting with you guys."

"Not a problem," Brody said, scraping the cards into a pile without glancing at them. His eyes still locked on Aiden, he nodded and tapped the deck on the table. "We'll be here when you're done."

"Yep, waiting to chitchat," Castillo said, holding his sock up in the air as if inspecting his lousy sewing. The eyes on the thing were lopsided, but it was actually start-ing to take on an eerie resemblance to Banks. Aiden made a mental note to refrain from pissing Auntie Castillo off.

"You said she's at the Joint Reception Center?" he asked Brody.

"Yep."

A nod of thanks and he headed out the door and across the base at a double-step.

What the hell was Sage doing here?

His guts were in knots, the emotions he'd been care-fully ignoring churning. Maybe it was news. Something she didn't want to tell him over the phone.

He'd just talked to the Professor two nights ago, so he

knew the older man was recovering from surgery well and they were pretty sure they'd got most of the cancer.

He'd had his thrice-weekly email update from Dr. Brooke this morning.

They wouldn't lie about Lee's health.

Sage must be here for a different reason.

The logical ones all ran through Aiden's mind and he let them run right back out. Because every one of them was tied to the emotional nightmare of their last encounter. But she wasn't a masochist. Nor had she outed their engagement to her father. He knew she hadn't because the Professor was still pitching job changes and property purchases.

So why ever she was here, he was sure it had nothing to do with logic.

He was equally sure his funk was about to take a nosedive, skating somewhere along heartache and misery.

He wondered what advice Castillo would have for that. A threesome with triplets, probably.

SAGE PACED. Five steps to the window wall, seven steps to the door, three steps to the lumpy couch, then do it all over again.

Nerves.

They sucked. She couldn't decide what she hated more. The miserable pain that was now her constant companion. The sense of loss in realizing that she'd finally found the answer to everything she'd been searching for, only to have to let it go. Or the giddy rush that had her skin dancing in anticipation of being near Aiden again.

Find the silver lining, Sage, she warned for the millionth time this month.

At least she'd found her bliss, and had mind-blowingly incredible sex. Lots and lots of it, too. There were plenty of people who went through life without either.

As far as silver linings went, it was pretty weak. But she had the rest of her life. She'd shore it up eventually.

Feeling a smidge better after that dreary pep talk, she took a deep, meditative breath. Zen. Find Zen.

She'd just about found it when the door opened.

She spun around, her Zen fizzling like a wet firecracker.

"Aiden," she said.

She'd rarely seen him in his military clothes. Fatigues tucked into gleaming black boots, a fitted T stretched over that gorgeous, rock-hard chest. A cap shading his gaze, and the glint of metal around his neck.

Oh, my. He was one sexy SEAL.

Suddenly a million doubts pounded through her mind, each one shaking its finger at her in warning. Aiden didn't know why she was here. She didn't have to follow through with her plan.

Instead, she could throw herself in his arms, declare her lust and beg him for a quickie. She glanced around the room. There was a chair, right there.

"Why are you here?"

Sage swallowed hard, mentally waving goodbye to that little fantasy. Might as well stick with the original plan since her sexy SEAL was clearly thrilled to see her.

"It's so good to see you, too," she said, not bothering to rein in her sarcasm. The ugly combination of heartbreak and sexual frustration tended to make her grumpy.

"What's the deal? Are you here to try and talk me into playing another round of Mission Marriage?"

Clearly he'd rather play with pygmy cannibals. Still, if she thought it'd get him into bed one more time, it might be worth rounding up a few short, hungry tribesmen.

As if she were starving herself and he was a feast, she stared at him. He only looked better now than he had when he'd told her he loved her. Given that he'd followed that declaration up by deeming them impossible, she shouldn't want to wrap her arms around that hard torso of his and squeeze.

"Sage?" he prompted impatiently.

"No more missions," she said. Then, pressing her lips together to keep them from shaking, she forced herself to say, "Actually, I'm here to break our engagement."

His eyes widened and for just a second he looked shocked. Hurt, even. Then he shook his head as if trying to dislodge her words.

"Break our engagement? The fake one?"

Sage sniffed. For a man who didn't do sarcasm very often, he was very good at it.

"Well, it's only fake to you and I," she pointed out. She tried to smile, but could only manage a tilt of her lips.

"But not to your father."

No. Her tilt fell away. But her father wouldn't want her to ruin Aiden's life by living a lie. Nor would he want her to be miserable spending her days and nights wishing that lie were real. Sage had been in—and out of—a lot of relationships. She'd thought herself in love at least a half-dozen times over the years. Now she knew better. With those, she'd easily gotten over the relationship within a week, easily able to ignore or dislike the beau in question.

But not Aiden. Despite his being the only person to ever break her heart, she couldn't feel badly toward him. Since ignoring him was proving impossible, too, she knew she needed to take drastic steps if she was going to get on with her life.

Her long, blissless life.

"I know we went into this for my father, but it's served its purpose," she told him.

"The purpose was to provide your father a positive

focus to help him get through treatments, to assist in his healing. How has that changed?"

Sage combed her fingers through her hair, wanting to tug on the long strands to relieve some of the frustration. This should be easy. She breaks up, he smiles in gratitude, they go their separate ways. Why was he arguing with her?

"Look, our engagement was good for my dad's spirits. But it's bad for you," she reasoned. There. Logic. Aiden should love that.

"How? I'm here, you're up there with your dad. I'm not seeing where this is a major pain in my ass."

Sage wanted to ask if missing her like crazy was a pain in his ass, but was afraid to hear that he hadn't missed her enough to even feel a twinge.

Stick with the plan, she told herself. She straightened her spine, pretending it was made of steel instead of mush, and took a deep breath. Get this done and get home.

"How many calls have you had from my father that included hints about leaving the service? Or beyond hints, that straight-out painted a picture of the happy professor life he's putting together for you."

He didn't have to say anything. The truth was right there on his face. He shrugged, though.

"I'm a big boy, Sage. I can deal with hints, requests and nagging just fine." He narrowed his eyes. "You came down here to break up with me because your dad is nagging? Ponied up plane fare, flew to San Diego, rented a car, finagled your way onto base. All to tell me that our make-believe engagement isn't working for you anymore."

He made it sound so stupid. And maybe if it'd just been the nagging, he'd have a point. But it was more. It was her peace of mind. Still, Sage couldn't resist correcting him.

"Actually, I borrowed Dad's car and drove down. I-5 is boring, but a pretty easy trip." At his dead-eyed stare, she blew out a breath, then lifted both hands in the air. "Don't you think breaking up by email is the epitome of tacky? And something that, if intercepted, would ruin the entire engagement mission. Don't you guys have rules against that kind of thing?"

"Sage?"

After a deep sigh, she pushed one hand through her hair, then shrugged.

"We need to end this. That's the only way we can get past it." Before he could argue, and he had a good one, she could tell from the stubborn look in his eyes, she held up one hand. "I don't want us to be a mess, Aiden. This whole thing, it got out of hand. If it keeps going, we're never going to be able to be friends again. We'll lose each other for good."

And she couldn't stand that thought.

She could deal with not having him in her bed. She could handle him not loving her. But she couldn't live without him in her life, even if it was just as a distant friend again.

"My dad's nagging has to be a distraction. And that's on top of you already being worried about his health. Drama between us will only cause you more stress, mess with your head. I don't want to be responsible for any of that." She swallowed hard and shrugged. "I couldn't live with myself worrying what that'd do to you. To your performance."

"So you're doing this for my, what? Safety? Peace of mind?" He shook his head, giving her an icy look. "Do you have a pacifier and baby blanket in that big purse of yours, too?"

"I'm sorry."

His glare was fierce, but she lifted her chin and stood her ground. After a solid, miserable minute-long stare-out, he finally sighed, rubbing both hands over his face.

"Fine. You want to end it, go ahead. Tell your dad I couldn't deal, tell him you're running off to join the circus. Do whatever you want."

"It's for the best," she promised brokenly. She gulped back the tears, reminding herself that crying made her blotchy and she didn't want him to see her that way. "You might be irritated with me now, but soon, probably as soon as tomorrow, you'll admit I'm right."

Sage winced at his dead-eyed stare, one that was just as lethal as some of the weapons he carried.

"Don't count on it," he said, heading for the door.

"Aiden?"

"What?" he asked, tossing a glare over his shoulder.

"Kiss me goodbye?" she suggested, unable to resist one last taste.

"Kiss you…" Aiden yanked off his hat, smacked it against his thigh, then crunched it in his fist so tight, she figured it was wrinkled for life.

He stormed over, looking so ferocious her toes melted.

His eyes never leaving hers, he grabbed her by the forearms, yanked her up and pressed his mouth over hers.

As soon as their lips touched, the anger melted away.

Passion, delight, and the most painful surge of love she'd ever felt washed through her with each slide of his lips.

Then he stopped. It was all Sage could do not to grab him back and hold on forever.

"There," he said, pulling away physically, and if the chill washing over her bare skin was any indication, emotionally. "There's your kiss goodbye. Have a fun life, Sage."

She tried to speak, but couldn't find her voice until he reached the door.

"Aiden," she called.

Hand on the doorknob, he froze but didn't look back.

She swallowed the painful knot of tears, then forced the words out.

"We're still friends, right?"

Her heart froze waiting for his response.

It seemed like forever before he dropped his head to his chest. Still not looking at her, he finally sighed.

"Yeah, Sage. We'll always be friends."

13

THIS SUCKED.

The warm overhead sunshine sucked.

The sound of the waterfall whooshing into the pool sucked.

The iced tea, the fresh fruit and even the gentle harp music she'd put on to soothe her sucked.

Sage lay on the chaise and sighed.

For the first time in her life, she'd done the responsible thing. She'd chased wisdom instead of pleasure. She'd put Aiden's safety over her heart.

It was the smart thing, the right thing to do.

Being smart, and right, sucked.

She should be happy. Her father was doing so much better. This new career idea of hers seemed to be panning out. And all she'd had to give up was the love of her life.

Of course, he'd given up on her way before she'd given up on them, so maybe she was beating herself up for no reason.

Sage threw one arm over her eyes, blocking the glow of the sun, and tried not to scream.

All week, she'd done this. Went round and round in mental circles, chasing one painful thought after the other.

Did she do the right thing, cutting the engagement off? Should she have tried to wear Aiden down with sexual promises and homemade cookies? Was keeping their friendship worth the cost of a broken heart? Wasn't keeping him safe worth everything?

Argh. She ground her teeth so tight, she tasted enamel.

Suddenly, footsteps echoed on the stone patio.

No. Not another well-meaning friend here to cheer her up. Or worse her father, checking up on her.

She couldn't take it.

Maybe if she lay there without moving, whoever it was would think she was asleep and go away.

"I know you're awake, so you might as well talk to me."

Oh, my God.

"Aiden?" Sitting bolt upright, she stared at the man next to her.

Was he real? Not a mirage brought on by sleep deprivation, sunstroke and dehydration brought on by crying for seven days straight?

She shaded her eyes and looked closer.

He looked real. And grumpy. His casual jeans and T were at odds with the power and authority of his stance.

She should probably worry that she found the grumpiness just as sexy as the power.

"What are you doing here?" she asked, not sure she wanted to know.

"It took me a week to figure out what you'd done," he told her, hands on his hips as he aimed that intense look her way.

"And you're supposed to be a genius?" she asked, trying to sound teasing but the words were too tight to come off as light as she wanted. "I told you face-to-face what I was doing. Should I have written it in a note, too?"

"You were trying to save me from myself. Just like you

initiated this engagement to save your dad from worrying. You do that a lot, Sage. You think you need to be the one doing all the sacrificing in a relationship."

That was ridiculous. Just because she always had been the one to sacrifice didn't mean she wanted it that way.

"I'm hardly a martyr."

"Nope. You might not take pleasure in suffering for others. But you do have a bad habit of suffering all the same."

Didn't she, though? Sage sighed, resisting the urge to drop her head into her hands. Still, there was suffering for the sake of drama, which she might have inadvertently given in to in the past. And there was sacrificing for the safety of someone she loved.

She didn't figure pointing that out would make Aiden leave any faster, though.

"Do you have a point?" she asked instead. "A reason you came back here when you should still be on duty?"

"Yeah. I'm here to fix this mess."

Sage made a show of looking around the pristine grounds and glistening pool.

"You might have wasted a trip."

"The mess that is us," he clarified.

Us? Why was he doing this to her? Sage's heart was one big ball of misery and her stomach tied in knots. She'd never thought Aiden was the type to torture the innocent.

"Aren't we over?" she asked, using her best *humoring the crazy man* tone. "Remember? We unofficially split weeks ago over champagne. Then we made it official last week when you were in your sexy SEAL clothes."

His lips twitched, either over the champagne or her still thinking him sexy.

"Nope. We've been together, in one form or another, for twenty years. Too long for us to end that easily."

Easily? She'd barely slept in weeks. She'd spent the first

week after he left with her face in bag after bag of M&M's, then the next two weeks miserably sick to her stomach and unable to eat. She'd had to resort to self-hypnosis to meet her publishing obligations and was almost ready to give up on even believing in her positive-thinking bio-feedback MP3s.

How the hell was any of that easy?

Luckily, either because he saw the look on her face or because he simply wanted to take advantage of her brief silence, he lifted a hand before she could say anything.

"You said you split up with me because your dad was pressuring me to leave the service. Right?" He didn't wait for her to confirm the obvious. "Did you argue the point with him? Despite his illness, I'm betting you did everything you could to convince him to give it up."

She shrugged.

He raised his brows, making it clear he wasn't going to let her brush off this conversation.

Fine, then. If they had to have it, they could do it fast, then he could leave again.

"Well, he was using me as justification for trying to get you to quit." She lifted both hands in the air as if it was obvious. "Of course I told him to let it go. I knew leaving the navy wasn't what you'd want to do."

"But he didn't let up."

"He quit nagging you when I told him we broke our engagement, didn't he?" He'd said he had, and her father never lied.

"Right. He quit nagging me." Giving her a searching look, Aiden grimaced. "As much pressure as he'd put on me, he was putting more on you. Pressure to get you to pressure me, I mean. You broke it off to get him off my back."

Seeing no point in confirming the obvious, she just shrugged.

"I broke it off because it was over," she said instead.

"You broke it off to save me from having to choose. To save me from worrying, from stressing over it." He looked as insulted as if she'd claimed he had a tiny dick. "Because this is you, Sage. It's what you do. You find an underdog, someone or something that needs you and fix or help them."

"You're not a homeless puppy, Aiden."

"No." He grimaced, then huffed out a deep breath. "I'm the man you love. The one you'd do anything for, even make yourself miserable instead of putting me through stress."

"You're being silly," Sage denied, scrambling out of the lounge chair and grabbing her cover-up. She was feeling a little too naked for this conversation. "We had an agreement, remember? Now that my dad looks to be out of danger, the agreement isn't necessary."

"Okay, yeah. You're right. That agreement served its purpose." Aiden clenched his jaw, then gave her a sharp nod. "Which is why I'm here. So we can negotiate a new agreement."

Sage wet her lips, her stomach jumping in so many directions she wasn't sure if she was excited, nervous or two breaths away from throwing up.

"I don't think so," she said quietly. She stepped around the chaise. The flimsy piece of pool furniture wasn't any obstacle for Aiden. But maybe it'd keep her from throwing herself into his arms. "I think we'd be better off sticking with my plan."

He pursed his lips, considering her words. Then he shook his head.

"Nope. I don't think we would."

"That's not fair. We haven't given my plan any time yet." She circled her hand in the air. "Let's give it a year, maybe two. Then if it doesn't seem to be working, we can talk about a different agreement."

"Why are you afraid?"

Because she didn't like being hurt. For the first time in her life, she'd found something she wanted so much that she was afraid to go for it. She'd found bliss with Aiden. She'd found contentment and joy. Then he'd taken it away.

"You don't even know what I'm going to suggest," he pointed out when she didn't say anything. "You've never rejected something out of hand before, Sage. You're all about fairness and balance and giving everything its chance. Remember?"

"It doesn't matter what the suggestion is," she told him. Suddenly not caring if she sounded like an idiot or a needy drama queen, she wrapped her hands around the edge of the chaise and leaned forward intently. "I can't do it, Aiden. I can't take the chance."

"Of what? Of us having a fight?" He frowned, his brows furrowed so tight they almost made a single line. "Or is it because I'm in the military? Are you afraid of committing to a SEAL? Is it the danger? Or the time apart?"

"No, of course not."

"Then what is your justification for walking away from the best thing in your life?"

"Fine." She threw her hands in the air. "You want to know why? Here it is."

She stormed around the chair, getting close enough to poke her finger into his chest.

"I can't go through this kind of thing again. We are wonderful together. We are perfect for each other. We understand each other inside and out. I know your fears, your hopes. I know how to make you smile. You not only understand, but appreciate my quirks, my needs."

"Right. And that's all bad because…"

"Because when we're together, we're everything I've been searching my entire life for," she yelled. "We're everything I want to spend the rest of my life nurturing, enjoying, reveling in."

He gave a slow nod.

"Not to be redundant, but again, why is that bad?"

"Because we can't have it," she said quietly. Suddenly, with no warning, her anger drained away, leaving her to blink away tears. "Because as fun as it is, sooner or later, you'll walk away."

"I…" His mouth opened and closed a couple of times. He shook his head, then gave her a narrow look. "I'm sorry. You think I'll be the one who walks away?"

The only way to convince him was to tell him the truth. The whole truth. No matter how much it hurt. Sage swallowed hard, then laying one hand on his wrist, she gazed up at him.

"You're a flake, Aiden."

He pressed his lips together, either to keep from laughing or cussing. But he didn't say a word, just inclined his head for her to continue.

"You don't make choices. Not long-term ones. You've taken enough college courses to get four degrees, but you won't declare a major. You're in the service, doing a job you love. But each time you only re-up for the minimum time allowed." She waved her hand. "You don't commit, Aiden."

She waited, sure he'd argue, or worse, laugh. But he just gave her a long look.

"So that's why you're afraid of this new agreement between us?" he asked quietly, turning his hand so their fingers entwined. Sage almost melted at the ease of the move, and forced herself to nod.

"Yeah. That's why. You're the answer to everything I've ever wanted." She lifted her free hand to stop his response when he opened his mouth. "But I don't want it temporarily. It's been hard enough trying to get over you this month. I can't do it again. And I can't do it again and again."

His frown was ferocious. For a second, he looked like he was going to argue. Then he gave a slow nod.

"Okay, that's fair. If anyone would recognize someone who's avoiding commitment, it'd be you."

"Cute," she muttered, tugging at her hand.

He wouldn't let go. Instead, he lifted it to his mouth, brushing his lips over her knuckle. This time she did melt. Why did he have to be gorgeous, smart *and* sweet? Damn him.

"And you're right. I'd actually come to the same conclusion last week."

What? Sage frowned, replaying his words.

"You did?"

"Nothing like night maneuvers in the freezing ocean to make a guy think seriously about his life."

Panic suddenly gripped her, all those melting happy feelings freezing in terror. Please, oh, please, don't let him be leaving the navy because of her. As much as she wanted to hear his next words, she didn't want to hear that.

"The day after you visited, I pulled together my credits, declared a major. It'll only take me a class or two to get my degree." He paused to brush a kiss over her mouth, which was hanging open in shock. "So I've got a couple of choices now. I can teach, like your dad wanted. Or I can stay in the navy, be an officer."

The panic grew teeth, gnawing and gnashing at her guts. Sage shook her head. It wasn't fair. She couldn't do this.

"You're not asking me to decide which you do, are you?"

"Nope. I already know what you'd say." He slid his hands over her waist, pulling her stiff body closer as if she wasn't showing any resistance. "That's why I'm here. That's why I want to renegotiate our deal."

Sage gazed up at him. He was so gorgeous. His hazel eyes shone and his smile was that same sweet curve of his lips that made her heart race. She wanted him so much. Wanted this, a real chance, for them so much.

Maybe he was right. Maybe she was a martyr. Because as wonderful as that would be, she couldn't do it at the cost of what he was meant to do.

"Aiden—"

"So here's the deal," he interrupted, sliding his hands over her butt to cup her cheeks and pull her against the temptation of his growing erection. She'd almost agree to anything for one more ride on that hard length. And he was offering her a lifetime ride pass. It was enough to make a strong woman weep. And she was feeling anything but strong.

"I want a long-term agreement. One that's a lot harder to get out of."

"Aiden—"

"I want us to get married. No engagement, since we already did that in fake form. Just married. Right away."

Oh, my.

Sage's heart did a wild dance, tears filling her eyes. She cupped his face in her hands, giving him a gentle smile. She loved him so much.

"Aiden—"

"You said you loved me. I know you, Sage, you wouldn't say it if you didn't mean it and if you meant it, a few weeks wouldn't change it." His words shot out like ammo from an automatic weapon. Fast, loud, forceful. "So…you'll marry me, right?"

"I can't," she said, the words almost choking her in unhappiness. "I can't. If we married, if you left the military and became Professor Masters, eventually you'd be miserable."

"You think I'd be miserable as a professor?"

She didn't know why he was looking at her so closely, but she felt like the fate of the world, or the two of their lives, rested on her next words. So she chose them carefully.

"I do love you. I think maybe, on some level, I always have." The ferocious look faded from his face, leaving smug male satisfaction. "But—"

"You can skip the but," he interrupted.

"But I can't do it. I can't let you give up a career that's perfect for you to chase a dream that, well, just doesn't fit." She winced, her thumbs rubbing over his cheekbones trying to offer comfort. "You're brilliant, Aiden. But you'd never be happy as a professor."

His stare was long and intense. Long and intense enough to make her spine start itching. Sage shifted, trying to accept that this was very likely goodbye. At least, for a few years until she'd gotten past this enough to be near him without wanting to strip naked and dance around his body.

"Interesting."

"Interesting, how?"

"Interesting that you'd say exactly what I knew you would," he told her with a wicked smile.

"You knew I'd…"

"Sage, I know you inside out. Better than I know myself, really. Out on those maneuvers when I was trying to figure out what I wanted to do, I finally realized the easiest way was to simply ask myself what you'd tell me to do."

"And you came up with marriage?" she asked, joy and excitement starting to creep in to smother the freak-out.

"Nah. I figured you'd tell me to stay in the military. That it's where I'm happiest, where I feel like I'm following my bliss. That's the term you use, right?"

Her heart was dancing so fast it almost beat out of her chest. Laughing, then nodded.

"So, yeah. The part about staying in the military, that I got thinking like you," he told her. And if the pained expression on his face was anything to go by, that hadn't been an easy task. "The marriage part, though, that was all me."

He stepped back, just enough that she missed the warmth of his body. His gaze locked on hers, he reached into his pocket and pulled out a box.

Sage's heart tumbled somewhere into her tummy, her breath catching while her pulse raced. She folded her hands together to keep from grabbing. Him, or the box, she wasn't sure which.

He looked so sure, so strong when he smiled and took her hand. His eyes were filled with so much love she almost melted right there and then.

"No games this time," he said quietly, flicking open the small velvet box with his thumb and holding it up so she could see the ring inside.

Her eyes filled with tears.

"Oh," she murmured. "It's so beautiful."

Twisted bands of gold were encrusted with aquamarines, wrapping around a glittering diamond.

"I had it made for you," he said, letting go of her hand to take out the ring before putting the box back in his pocket.

He took her again, lifting it to his lips and brushing a soft kiss over her knuckles.

"I love you, Sage. I want us to spend our lives together, to grow old together, to build a family together." He took a deep breath, nudging the ring against her finger but not sliding it on. "Will you marry me?"

"Yes," she said softly, her heart in that single word.

He slipped the ring on her finger, barely giving her time to stare at it before his mouth covered hers. Their kiss was gentle, sweet and filled with promise.

Slowly he pulled back and gave her smile.

"This is going to be great," he said.

Sage wouldn't have been surprised if a rainbow arched overhead, landing at their feet while doves circled and flowers sang. Happiness, bigger than anything she'd ever felt in her life, wrapped around her as tightly as Aiden's arms.

"You're staying in the military?"

"Yep. At least until I retire."

"And you don't care what I do for a career?"

"As long as you're happy."

"And you're sure you want to get married?"

"I do." He grinned. "See, I even have the words right."

She'd thought she'd found bliss before? Clearly, she'd had no clue just how amazing bliss felt. Sage blinked fast to clear the tears from her eyes. She didn't want anything in the way of seeing his face right now.

"Well, since you've got the right words, I guess I should make sure mine are right, too." She swallowed, hard, then stepped up on tiptoe to brush her lips over his. "I do, too."

"Monday."

"What?"

"I told you, we've already done the engagement thing. I want to be married before I go back on duty and I only have a three-day pass."

Sage burst into delighted laughter.

"I guess I'm not the impulsive one in this relationship any longer," she realized, loving that.

"Maybe not." He swept her into his arms, his mouth taking hers in a hot, wild kiss that made her toes curl. When he finally lifted his head, his grin told her that was just the beginning. "But I promise that for the rest of your life, you'll be the happy one."

"The rest of my life?" she breathed, filled with joy.

"The rest of our lives," he promised.

And that, she realized joyfully, was bliss.

* * * * *

#795 DOUBLE TAKE
Unrated! • by Leslie Kelly

When her study on orgasms becomes talk-show fodder, researcher Lindsey Smith needs to hide from the gossip. But Mike Santori, the hunky new police chief, has a way of making Lindsey reveal all of her secrets...and give in to her deepest desires.

#796 SEDUCE ME
It's Trading Men! • by Jo Leigh

According to his trading card, steady, marriage-minded—and gorgeous!—Max Dorset sounds tailor-made for Natalie Gellar. But when they meet, she realizes Max is only interested in a good time with no strings attached!

#797 MAKE ME MELT
The U.S. Marshals • by Karen Foley

Jason Cooper broke Caroline Banks's young heart, and she's determined he won't get a second chance. But when the U.S. Marshal strides back into her life, looking hotter than ever, she wonders if her carefully guarded heart will be able to withstand the heat....

#798 WILD WEEKEND
by Susanna Carr

After a fantasy-fulfilling weekend in Vegas, it's back to reality for bank manager Christine Pearson—until she discovers sexy Travis Cain has arrived in town and wants to continue their shocking fling!

HBCNM0414

REQUEST YOUR FREE BOOKS!
2 FREE NOVELS PLUS 2 FREE GIFTS!

HARLEQUIN

Blaze®

red-hot reads!

HB13R2

Double Take

Suddenly the ferry lurched again, making him glad for his
strong grip on the railing. But the woman—Lindsey—wobbled
on her feet and, for a second, he thought she'd fall. Not even
thinking about it, he stepped into her path and grabbed her
before she could stumble.

Their legs tangled, hips bumped and chests collided. He
had a chance to suck in a shocked—and pleased—breath,
when her fine red hair whipped across his face, bringing with
it a flowery fragrance that cut through the briny air and went
right to his head. Just like this woman was doing.

"Whoa," she murmured, either because of the stumbling
or the fact that so much of her was now touching so much
of him.

"I've got you," he said, placing a firm hand on her shoulder. He turned his back to the wind, staying close, but giving
her some distance and disengaging the more vulnerable parts
of their bodies. As nice as she had felt pressed against him, he
didn't want her to know that his lower half was ignoring his
brain's order to be a polite protector and was instead going

straight for horny man. Their new position removed the danger of sensual overload, but also kept her blocked from the worst of the wind. "I won't let you fall overboard. Now glove up."

Not taking no for an answer, he lifted one of her small, cold hands and shoved a glove on it. He forced himself to focus only on the fact that her lips now had a bluish tint, not that they were pretty damned kissable. And that her expression was pure misery, not that her face was shaped like a perfect heart, with high cheekbones and a pointy, stubborn little chin.

Once her hands were adequately protected, she stepped the tiniest bit closer, as if welcoming the shelter of his body. Mike heaved in a deep breath of cold lake air, but found it tasted of spicy-fragranced woman.

Nice. Very nice.

She licked her lips. "So you're single, too?"

He noticed she didn't add *available,* maybe because she didn't want to sound like she was interested, though he could tell she was; but he recognized desire when he saw it. During those few moments when she'd landed hard against him, heat had flared between them, instinctive and powerful.

"I'm *very* single."

Pick up DOUBLE TAKE by Leslie Kelly, available this May wherever you buy Harlequin® Blaze® books.

HBEXP79799

This unexpected hunk might be just what she needs!

According to his trading card, steady, marriage-minded—and gorgeous!—Max Dorset sounds tailor-made for Natalie Gellar. But when they meet, she realizes Max is only interested in a good time with no strings attached!

Don't miss the latest in the *It's Trading Men!* miniseries,

Seduce Me
by *Jo Leigh*

Available May 2014 wherever you buy Harlequin Blaze books.

Available now from the
It's Trading Men! miniseries by Jo Leigh:

Choose Me
Want Me
Have Me

Too hot to handle!

Jason Cooper broke Caroline Banks's young heart, and she's determined he won't get a second chance. But when the U.S. marshal strides back into her life looking hotter than ever, she wonders if her carefully guarded heart will be able to withstand the heat....

From the reader-favorite miniseries
The U.S. Marshals

Make Me Melt
by *Karen Foley*

Available May 2014 wherever you buy
Harlequin Blaze books.

Don't miss *Hard to Hold,* already available from
The U.S. Marshals by Karen Foley.

⊕HARLEQUIN®

Blaze®

Red-Hot Reads
www.Harlequin.com

HB79801